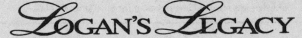

LOGAN'S LEGACY

WHAT A MAN NEEDS
PATRICIA THAYER

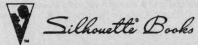

Silhouette Books

Published by Silhouette Books
America's Publisher of Contemporary Romance

Special thanks and acknowledgment are given to Patricia Thayer for her contribution to the LOGAN'S LEGACY series.

 SILHOUETTE BOOKS

ISBN 0-373-61397-0

WHAT A MAN NEEDS

Visit Silhouette Books at www.eHarlequin.com

Printed in U.S.A.

"Hell, woman, I haven't had a decent night's sleep since I met you!"

She stared at him, anger flashing in her eyes. "And that's my problem? You're blaming me for your lack of sleep? That's just great." She marched up the stairs, her shapely bottom swaying back and forth, heightening his desire. "Good night, Patrick. Sweet dreams," she taunted as she disappeared into her room. The door slammed behind her.

Patrick closed his eyes. Cynthia had him tied up in so many knots that he wasn't going to survive another day—another minute, another second. He climbed the stairs two at a time and stormed to her room.

Cynthia swung open the door and before she knew what hit her, Patrick grabbed her and pulled her to him.

"If you have any protests, you'd better tell me now, because I'm going to make love to you and I'm not stopping until I get my fill."

Cynthia reached up and ran her fingers through his hair. "No. You're not stopping until I get *my* fill."

PATRICIA THAYER

has been writing for eighteen years and has published twenty books with Silhouette. Her books have been nominated for the National Readers' Choice Award, Virginia Holt Medallion and a prestigious RITA® Award. In 1997, *Nothing Short of a Miracle* won the *Romantic Times* Reviewers' Choice Award for Best Special Edition. In 2002, *The Princess Has Amnesia!* won the Orange Rose for Best Traditional Romance. Pat says she really enjoyed working on LOGAN'S LEGACY. Her story is explosive from the start when stubborn rancher Patrick Tanner meets beautiful actress Cynthia Reynolds. And when she moves into his world, he doesn't stand a chance.

Thanks to the understanding men in her life—her husband of thirty-three years, Steve, and her three grown sons and three grandsons—Pat has been able to fulfill her dream of writing romance. Another dream is to own a cabin in the mountains, where she can spend her days writing and her evenings with her favorite hero, Steve. She loves to hear from readers. You can write to her at P.O. Box 6251, Anaheim, CA 92816-0251, or check her Web site at www.patriciathayer.com for her upcoming books.

Be a part of

LOGAN'S LEGACY

*Because birthright has its privileges
and family ties run deep.*

**When a cowboy meets an actress, neither
expects the fireworks their chemistry
ignites. Will their sweet passion lead to
everlasting love?**

Patrick Tanner: A no-nonsense cowboy with
a chip on his shoulder, Patrick threw caution to
the wind and entertained a beautiful movie star
on his ranch. They forgot their cares and indulged
in each other. Was this just the beginning of
something special?

Cynthia Reynolds: After years in Hollywood,
Cynthia felt her star was fading. So she came home
to escape and fell hard for hard-working, hard-loving
Patrick Tanner. He didn't care who she was—only
that she let him treasure her for as long as they had
together.

The Mysterious Wife: Carrie Martin had loved
Dr. Richie, but when he became a celebrity, their
marriage fell apart. Now, Carrie was determined to
confront the man she'd once adored and show him
what their love had produced.

THE SOLUTION YOU'VE BEEN WAITING FOR...

THE REMEDY YOU DESERVE...

NoWAIT

THE AMAZING NEW DIET OIL. USE IT AND WATCH THE POUNDS MELT AWAY!

NoWait: A little rub on the skin, and in no time you're thin!

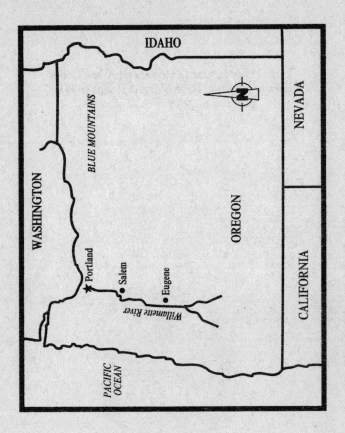

To the other *Logan's Legacy* Ladies, Cara Colter, Donna Clayton, Raye Morgan. It was truly a pleasure to work with all of you.

Prologue

"You have to believe you can do it," Dr. Richard Strong said to the crowded room. He paced in front of the podium at the Healthy Living Clinic in Portland, Oregon. "To be willing to change your lifestyle. It's not just with what you eat, but with how you feel about yourself. NoWait will only work if *you're* willing to work."

Richie knew he had every person in the room. It had taken years to perfect his presence, and the effort was finally paying off. Oh, yeah, he was good, especially at getting women's attention.

They had been the main contributors to his success and would do anything to get close to him, to show their gratitude. But that didn't stop the men from attending his seminars. From construction workers to doctors, they were buying his homeopathic oil…and making him rich.

And he believed he was changing their lives for the better.

Cynthia Reynolds sat in the back of the room with her sister, Kelly. Cynthia, too, was excited by Dr. Richie's talk. At thirty-five, she'd seen the changes in her body and she was aware of every extra pound. Not to mention that the camera picked up every tiny line on her face. In Hollywood, it was youth and beauty that stayed on top.

Her sister leaned toward her and whispered, "Do you really believe this homeopathic mumbo-jumbo?"

Kelly, two years younger, had a fresh, natural look. She had gone into law and made a name for herself here in Portland.

"I don't have a choice," Cynthia admitted.

Her sister smiled. "Then buy a truckload of this NoWait stuff."

"I only need a little behind my ears."

"Then do it and let's go hit the nightlife. I need to see a man about a horse."

One

Patrick Tanner walked into Morgan's Pub and squinted to adjust to the dim light. The room had a long oak bar on one side, and several booths on the other. The sound of clinking glasses and laughter was muffled by the loud music coming from the jukebox.

The place was already crowded with Friday-night customers.

Patrick continued to look around. There were several women who returned an I'm-interested look, but he didn't reciprocate. Not tonight. His youngest sister, Nora, had called and said she needed to see him. And anyone who knew Patrick knew his family came first, even if he had to drive forty miles from the ranch into Portland.

A long, thirsty drive, he thought as he walked to the bar and sat down on the stool. The burly bartender was wiping his hands on a towel when he came up to him. "What'll it be?"

"A beer. Whatever's on tap."

The man nodded, then took a mug from the shelf, tilted it under the spout and pulled the lever. Once the golden liquid had filled the glass to the brim, he set it down on the bar. "Enjoy."

"Thanks, I will." Patrick gripped the handle and took a long swallow. He didn't drink often, but a beer once in a while didn't hurt. He would never let alcohol consume his life. He'd never be like his father. Never.

Patrick pushed aside the bitter thoughts and glanced at his watch. Nora should have been here by now. He was reaching for his cell phone when the door opened and two women walked in. A blonde and a redhead, both unfamiliar, walked toward an empty table, both tall and beautiful enough to turn just about every man's head in the room. Patrick usually preferred blondes, but this time the redhead drew all his attention. She had striking features, large dark eyes, a wide, kissable mouth….

He changed his focus to her attire, a blue-green blouse and a pair of jeans that encased long, slender legs. When she turned around and his gaze dropped to her shapely bottom, Patrick took a long drink of his cold beer. Oh, boy, he'd been spending too much time on the ranch.

Cynthia Reynolds had wanted to argue with Kelly when she'd suggested coming to Morgan's Pub, and now, seeing the good-looking man at the bar, she was glad she hadn't.

Cynthia guessed his age at about thirty-five. He was a little rough around the edges with shaggy dark blond hair that hadn't seen a stylist in a long time. He wore a chambray shirt and a pair of jeans, faded and soft from wear, and a brown belt that circled his slim waist. Cyndi found she was daydreaming about how she would pop open each snap on his shirt….

She quickly pushed aside the thought. What was wrong with her? He wasn't even her usual type.

But when his gaze met hers, she couldn't seem to turn away. Those piercing eyes held her prisoner as a slow smile emphasized his already sensual mouth, and her breath suddenly locked in her lungs.

"See anything that interests you?" Kelly's voice broke through her reverie.

Cynthia hated that her sister could always read her so easily. Maybe that was the reason Kelly was such a good lawyer. She was not only beautiful, with her dazzling brown eyes and golden hair, but she'd also got the brains of the family.

"Maybe, but I'm not going to do anything about it."

The waitress came by for their drink order. Once it was given, their conversation started up again. "And what's wrong with having a little fun?" Kelly asked. "You can't work all the time. Besides, so far, no one has recognized you."

Cynthia was glad that people weren't asking for her autograph. She didn't want to be front cover in the tabloids, whether she did anything crazy or not.

"Maybe because I'm old news and I haven't actually been in a box-office hit in three years." Back then Cynthia Reynolds had had to turn movie scripts away.

"And that's going to change."

"Please don't tell me you set me up with a guy."

"No, I wouldn't do that." Kelly brushed back

her shoulder-length hair and glanced around the bar. "I'm looking for my assistant, Nora. She's going to help us with your problem."

"My problem? What problem?"

Kelly's eyes narrowed in disdain. "The problem you've had since you were six years old. Your fear of horses."

"What does that have to do with anything?"

"You've got to overcome that fear if you want to land the best movie role that's come down the pike in years."

Cynthia sighed. "You've been talking to Bernie."

Bernie Schwartz, her agent for the last fifteen years—and a veritable tiger when it came to the business. For the past two months, Bernie had been bugging her about this project.

"Is this about the Western, *Cheyenne?*" Cynthia asked.

"Of course it is," Kelly said as the waitress returned with their drinks. "From what I hear, you're perfect for the female lead."

Cynthia frowned. "They're looking for someone under thirty."

"So, you can pass for thirty," Kelly said convincingly.

Plus five years, Cynthia said to herself. "Not in

close-ups." She glanced toward the bar again. The man was still watching her. He nodded to her, then took a drink from his glass. Cynthia found herself lifting her own drink and nodding back, a flush heating her cheeks. What had gotten into her? She didn't flirt with strange men. But there was something about this cowboy that got her blood pumping. And that hadn't happened for a long time.

"It's so not fair," Kelly said, "especially when you know that the male lead will probably be at least thirty-five. That's discrimination. Just say the word and I'll—"

"No! That won't help my situation," Cynthia insisted. "It's bad enough that lately my phone hasn't exactly been ringing off the hook for roles. I'm sure a lawyer screaming discrimination will silence it totally."

Kelly had a successful practice as a divorce lawyer in Portland and she had always fought for the underdog. "Then how about a more subtle approach?"

Cynthia was having trouble concentrating. Her cowboy at the bar was too distracting. "And just what would that be?"

"You learn how to ride a horse and go after this role." She raised a hand. "And before you get all worked up, just hear me out. Nora has assured me that you can overcome your fear if you have the right teacher."

Cynthia's attention strayed to the bar again as a tingle ran through her. She wouldn't mind if this man taught her a few things.

"Cyndi, are you hearing anything I'm saying?"

"Sure I am. You think I should learn to ride."

Kelly looked toward the bar, then back at Cynthia with a smile. "My sister has good taste. So what's stopping you? Go talk to him. Just don't forget that we're going to be meeting with Nora in a little while."

"I can't promise that I'll get on a horse, Kelly, but I'll talk to her."

Cynthia stood and made her way across the room. She told herself she was crazy to do this, but her heart still raced. Her attraction to this man was not to be denied. As she got closer, that thought was the only thing that kept her from running in the other direction. That and his eyes were a brilliant, mesmerizing blue. His smile, she noticed, was slightly off center, only adding to his appeal. Her knees weakened as he stood up and pulled out the stool next to his.

She sat down. "Hi," she said breathlessly.

Patrick had been crazy to encourage this woman. Any minute his sister could walk in and he would have to end things. And he definitely wanted to spend time with this tall, gorgeous woman.

"Hi, yourself. I haven't seen you in here before," he said, wishing he could come up with something more clever.

She leaned in close so he could hear her, and he caught a whiff of her intoxicating perfume. "I'm from out of town," she offered as she stuck out her slender hand. "I'm Cyndi."

He clasped her small palm in his and immediately felt a warm, sexual charge. He nearly forgot his name. "Patrick."

Again she leaned in and gave a smile that had him forgetting everything. "Nice to meet you, Patrick."

He didn't release her hand, liking how it fitted into his. She didn't seem to object. "It's nice to meet you, too." Suddenly his ringing cell phone broke the spell. "Excuse me." He pulled it from his pocket and saw that it was his sister. Great, this woman not only made him forget his name but his sister. "Where are you?"

"That's what I'm calling about, Patrick. I had a flat tire."

"Tell me where you are and I'll come and fix it."

"No, it's already done. I did it myself. But I'm a mess so I'm on my way back to my apartment. I know you have a long drive back to the ranch, so I didn't want to hold you up."

"I thought you needed to talk."

"I do, but tomorrow's Saturday, so I'll just come out to the ranch and we'll talk then. Is that okay?"

Patrick looked over his shoulder at the sexy redhead beside him. "Sure. I'll look forward to it."

"Patrick, I'm going to be bringing along a friend and…I want you to keep an open mind."

Suddenly Cyndi's body brushed against him as she made room for more people at the bar. He felt a stirring in his gut and he had to work to keep focused on what Nora was saying. "So I'll see you then. As you can tell, Morgan's is noisy as usual." He said good-bye and pocketed the phone.

Cyndi's dark, questioning gaze met his. "Your wife?"

He shook his head. "My sister. I'm not married. How about you?"

Smiling, she shook her head and it nearly did him in. There was no way in hell he was going to let her slip away. He tilted his head toward hers to say something, but suddenly the jukebox came to life with another song and patrons raised their voices to be heard. "How long will you be in town?"

She shrugged. "About ten days," she shouted. "I'm visiting my sister." She nodded toward the woman at the table. This was perfect. Maybe they could spend some time together while Cynthia was in Portland.

"What do you say we go some place where we can hear ourselves talk?" He found he was holding his breath waiting for an answer.

"Do you know of such a place?"

Hell, he hadn't done anything like this in years. "There's a quiet lounge just down the street at the Grand Hotel. We could walk there from here."

Amazing herself, Cynthia nodded in agreement. Now she just had to convince Kelly that she was perfectly sane. "Just let me tell my sister where I'll be."

She walked back to the table to find her sister wasn't alone. Two men were seated with her and she seemed engrossed in conversation. Cynthia took her aside. "Would you mind if I go and have a quiet drink with Patrick?"

"Cyndi, you don't have to ask for permission. Besides, he's sexy as hell. It's about time you had some fun."

Cynthia blushed. "We're just going to the lounge at the Grand Hotel."

"Then go for it. Nora just called and apologized for not being here. She had car trouble. So we rescheduled for tomorrow, and she wants us to come out to her family's ranch. She insists if anyone can help you with your fear of horses, it's her brother." Kelly cocked an eyebrow. "That means I'm coming by your hotel early."

Cynthia didn't want to talk about her fears or her fading career now. "Fine, then I'll see you tomorrow." She walked to the door and to Patrick. Tonight she wanted to get lost in this cowboy's eyes.

Patrick walked through the front door of the historic hotel, following close behind his beautiful date. He'd been to the bar here before, and it was still pretty lively, though a lot quieter than Friday night at Morgan's Pub.

What he wanted mostly was to find somewhere he could be alone with Cyndi. But the tall, statuesque beauty seemed to draw stares everywhere and she seemed almost shy with the attention. Once inside the lounge, he directed her to a small table in the corner where the light was dim and they could talk without shouting at each other.

He ordered her a glass of wine, and he had another beer. The sound of jazz came through the speakers, but they could at least carry on a conversation. Once the drinks arrived, Patrick had lost his thirst for a cold beer. He wanted Cyndi, and when her hot gaze locked with his, he had no doubt she wanted the same. She leaned forward and whispered, "So, where do we go from here, Patrick?"

Patrick's eyes never left hers as he closed the short distance between them and covered her mouth with his. *Intoxicating. Sweet. Tempting.* They were the words that described this woman. Finally he broke off the kiss.

"I think I should just call you Cyn. As in pure sin. That's what you are. And you've been driving me crazy since you walked into Morgan's."

"Well, stop wasting time and just kiss me—" The last of her words were swallowed as he captured her mouth once again. This time he ran his tongue over her lips, then delved inside to taste her, mimicking what he wanted to do to her. He released her and sucked much-needed air into his lungs as his lips moved to her ear to nibble. Feeling her shiver, he then returned to her incredible mouth. "I want you."

The sound of laughter caused them to break off the kiss, and Cyndi buried her head against his neck and whispered, "We just can't seem to find any place to be alone. Maybe we should go upstairs."

Patrick froze momentarily as Cyndi raised her head, her whiskey-brown eyes showing her desire. "Oh, baby, don't tease, I want you too badly."

"I'm not teasing." She ran her fingers over his chest. "I want you to make love to me."

"Give me ten minutes to make the arrangements." Patrick kissed her quickly, then pulled away. "I'll meet you in the lobby."

Patrick had no idea what he'd done to deserve this night, he thought as he handled the check-in. He quickly stopped by the hotel gift shop and picked up some protection. He might be out of his mind for this woman, but he wasn't crazy. Yes, he was. That was the only thing that explained his impulsive actions, but when he walked back to the lobby to find Cyndi standing by the elevators, all rational thoughts disappeared from his head.

Silently, they rode up to the sixth floor, then got off. Patrick took her hand and laced it with his, and together they walked down the long hall, her body brushing against his and causing an unbearable tingling. Suddenly he pulled her into the ice-machine alcove and took her mouth in a heated kiss.

"Are you sure you want this?"

"I'm sure."

Her hands moved over his chest and he groaned, then with her arms wrapped against him, they continued their journey. Locating their room, Patrick used the key card and opened the door, allowing Cyndi to go in first. He followed and closed the door behind him. When he turned around, Cyndi pushed him back against the door as her lips met his.

He drank from her sensual mouth, hungry for more. His hands were busy as he ravished her body, and by the time they moved to the bed, her blouse and bra were gone, as was his shirt.

"You're beautiful," he said as he worshiped her perfect breasts. Then he dipped his head and laved the hard bud. She whimpered as she held his head against her chest.

Cynthia had never felt like this before. She'd never been so sexually aware of a man, or so aggressive. She couldn't seem to stop herself as her hands raked over Patrick's perfectly sculpted body. She went to the zipper on his jeans and tugged it down. He only grinned as he helped her remove his pants.

He stood before her naked. He was perfect. She raised a shaky hand and began to trace his skin on his broad chest, following the swirl of sandy hair that dipped past his waist to his erection. He felt his breathing grow rapid as her hands worked their magic.

Patrick had to stop her. "You *are* sin." He grabbed her hands. "My turn." He opened her zipper and pulled down her jeans. Cynthia kicked off her heeled sandals then stepped out of her pants. With a long, appreciative stare, he finally pressed her back on the bed, causing her fiery hair to flare out against the pillow.

He grabbed a condom from the box and prepared himself, then came to her. He grinned down at her, one small part of him hoping he survived this night. The rest of him not caring. He'd die a happy man. Suddenly he became serious as his desire for her turned to desperation. His hands moved over her body, then between her legs, slipping inside to see that she was wet and ready for him.

"Please, Patrick, I want you," she cried, squirming against him, her desire and excitement showing in her eyes.

He moved against her body, then whispered in her ear. "I'm going to fill every inch of you, Cyndi," he promised as he nudged himself between her legs, slipping into her inch by inch.

Cyndi raised her hips and he pushed into her again and again. The bed jerked against the wall, but he didn't stop. He couldn't, Cyndi wouldn't let him. He growled as his hips moved against her writhing body. He plunged and withdrew until he felt her tighten around him. With the next thrust she cried out his name, triggering his climax. He drove into her one more time, then he exploded.

With a groan he collapsed onto her and Cyndi held him close. "That was incredible," he said.

"Not bad for starters," she whispered.

Patrick raised his head to catch her teasing smile. "I'm going to make you sorry you said that." He tickled her ribs and she began to squirm.

"Stop! Stop!" she begged.

He paused. "I thought you wanted more."

"Then let me clarify that." She moved against him. "Stop tickling me. Don't stop touch-ing…kissing…tasting…loving me."

"My pleasure." He leaned down and, starting at the top of her sexy body, began to work his way through the list.

Sometime early the next morning, Cynthia re-alized two things—she was naked in a strange bed, and she wasn't alone. Her eyes shot open. It was still dark, or at least it was in the room. And the man softly snoring against her ear was the same one she'd had incredible sex with last night…and at two o'clock and again at four. She glanced at the clock to see it was now 5:34 a.m.

She drew a calming breath, but it didn't help. She drew another and slipped from the bed. She picked her clothes off the floor, quickly put them on and slipped on her shoes, all the while praying that Patrick wasn't going to wake up.

With her purse in hand, she headed for the door, then paused, hating to leave without saying a word. But what could she say—thanks for the night of incredible sex? And as far as she knew, Patrick didn't know who she was and she'd like to keep it that way. He took Cyndi to bed, not Cynthia Reynolds. Some things should be left alone.

With a glance over her shoulder, Cynthia allowed herself the pleasure of seeing the near-naked man in bed. He'd been a wonderful lover, but she couldn't take the chance of spending any more time with this man. Not that she wouldn't like to, but she had her career to think about.

Cynthia turned and walked out the door. Keeping her head down, she joined an older couple on the elevator. When the woman's eyes showed recognition, Cynthia tensed.

"Say, are you that actress… What's her name? Cynthia Reynolds?"

Cynthia shook her head. "You know, I get that all the time. Myself, I don't see it." The doors to the lobby opened and Cynthia made her getaway.

She hailed a cab back to her hotel. Luckily, she used a private entrance and could get to her private suite without anyone stopping her, wanting to know where she'd been or where she was going. She only had to face her sister in a few hours and convince her that she hadn't done anything last night that she regretted.

She might have been stupid to make love with Patrick last night, but she'd never regret it.

Two

With a groan, Patrick rolled over in bed, his mind filled with erotic images. He blinked, suddenly recalling the sexy woman he'd made love to nearly all night long.

Cyndi. Patrick smiled as he reached out for her, but he found the other side of the bed empty; just her scent lingering on the pillow. He sat up and glanced around the dark room only to discover he was alone. He swung his legs over the side of the mattress. His clothes were still scattered where he'd tossed them, but there was no sign of Cyndi's things. He got up and walked to check the bathroom. It was deserted, too.

There was no trace of her anywhere. He sank against the doorjamb. "Looks like you've been dumped." Not that he'd had much experience in taking women to hotel rooms, but he hadn't seen this coming. Especially after what they'd shared last night…just hours ago. It was a blow to his ego, he admitted to himself. He wasn't planning on carrying this attraction that far anyway, but she didn't need to run away.

He felt his anger grow as he slipped on his briefs and jeans. Well, the hell with her. He didn't need the complication anyway. He had the ranch to worry about and it was going to take all his attention when he expanded the vineyard. He sat down and pulled on his boots. And Cyndi No-last-name didn't fit into those plans. She'd probably done him a favor by leaving. No awkward moments. No regrets. He wasn't into commitment anyway. Not with the possibility he might inherit his father's bad habits. Besides, he'd already raised a family—his three sisters. He finally had time to himself.

It had taken him a lot of years to turn the Tanner Ranch into a profitable operation. Added to the cattle, and the breeding and training of horses, he had the Christmas tree farm to watch over. And his dream of the Tanner Vineyard would take all his time and energy, not to mention the money he still had to come up with. Since he didn't want to use any of the equity in the ranch, he'd been saving every penny.

So he didn't need distracting thoughts about tall sexy, auburn-haired women. He ran his fingers through his hair and headed out the door. Last night was a night he needed to forget.

Problem was, he doubted he ever would.

The pounding sound grew louder. Cynthia rolled over in bed, hoping it would go away.

"Cyndi, open the door," her sister called.

Cynthia groaned. She climbed out of bed, went to the door and pulled it open.

"Good, you're awake," her sister said as she swept into the large hotel suite.

One of the reasons Cynthia always stayed in a hotel when she visited Portland was so she could have her own space and privacy. What a joke.

Cynthia glanced at the clock. "It's seven-thirty in the morning. What are you doing here at this ungodly hour?"

"That's right. And you aren't dressed." Kelly examined her. "Looks like you partied a little too hearty last night. How'd it go with the sexy cowboy?"

Cynthia stiffened. "Fine. We had a few drinks and some laughs," she said. And made love three times, she added silently. "Don't change the subject. What are you doing here?"

Kelly's eyes narrowed as she folded her arms. "How could you forget that we're going out to the Tanner Ranch. You have a date with a nice horse."

Cynthia groaned. "Not this morning."

"Yes, this morning. I told Nora we'd be out at the ranch early, so go get dressed."

"Well, call and tell her we'll make it another time."

Kelly took Cyndi's hand, led her to the sofa and sat her down. "Look, sis, you told me you wanted a chance at that movie. And the only way to get it is to show you can handle a horse. Has that changed since last night?"

Career had always come first for Cyndi, and somehow over the years, it had become her life. Every serious relationship she'd tried had gone sour when she had to go off on location, or the guy couldn't handle her kissing her leading men, especially when the tabloids blew it up as more. And she'd never met any man who had meant enough to her to give it all up. Yet, last night…Patrick had been the first one in a long time who'd made her think how nice it would be to have someone in her life.

But in the early morning light, she'd panicked.

"Nothing has changed. Give me twenty minutes to get showered and dressed."

"Not a problem. I'll call room service for some coffee." Kelly went to the phone, speaking over her shoulder to Cynthia, "Put on some jeans. I have two pairs of boots for you in the car."

"Why do I feel like I've been had?"

Kelly turned and smiled. "I'm just giving you a little push. You're a damn good actress and you deserve the part in *Cheyenne*. I just want to make sure you have every opportunity to get it."

Cynthia stepped into the large bathroom and turned on the shower. She knew getting the female lead in the movie could jump-start her fading career. She only hoped that Nora's brother knew what he was doing and had a very gentle horse.

Once in the car, Cynthia thought of a dozen excuses not to go through with this. Right up to the time they drove under the archway to the Tanner Ranch.

The beautiful, serene area seemed to stretch for miles. Against the mountains in the distance, everything was lush and green, still damp from an early-morning shower. White split-rail fences lined either side of the road, and several horses and foals roamed freely in the pastures.

A large yellow two-story house with white shutters came into view. The huge porch was adorned with hanging baskets of colorful flowers, and a swing faced a spectacular view of pine-covered mountains. Kelly drove on and headed to the barn. The white structure had a charcoal-colored roof and huge framed doors that stood open. A man walked out leading a very large horse. Cynthia's heart began to pound in her chest.

"Come on, let's go find Nora," Kelly said.

"Let's try the house first," Cynthia suggested, not yet ready to get near a horse.

Just as they got out of the car, a brunette woman exited the house—Nora Tanner, she assumed, from her friendly wave to Kelly. She was about twenty-five and had a petite, shapely body clad in jeans and a cotton T-shirt.

"Hi, Kelly," the woman said, then turning to Cynthia, she gushed, "Oh, Ms. Reynolds, it's such a pleasure to meet you."

"Oh, no, an adoring fan." Kelly rolled her eyes.

Cynthia ignored her. "Please, call me Cyndi."

Nora nodded. "Cyndi. I'm so glad you could make it."

"I'm sure my sister told you that I don't do very well around horses."

"I'm sorry to hear that, but I'm happy that you're going to give riding another chance," Nora offered. "Welcome to the Tanner Ranch."

Cynthia heard a horse's high-pitched whinny. "I'm not sure this is going to work."

"But you're here to try," Nora said.

Cynthia nodded reluctantly.

"Good, you won't be sorry. My brother is the best with horses, and the best teacher. Let's go find him." She headed toward the barn.

Cynthia reluctantly followed her. How could she have let herself be talked into this? Nora went on ahead and talked to a man with dark brown hair and hazel eyes who looked to be in his late thirties. Just their flirtatious demeanor told her they weren't brother and sister.

"This is Forest. He's the foreman here. Forest, this is Kelly and Cyndi."

The cowboy raised his fingers to his hat in a salute. "It's nice to meet you, ladies."

Cyndi managed a hello, but was watching the horse in the corral. The shiny coal-black stallion wasn't docile like the horses she'd seen in the pasture. This animal was prancing around, bobbing his head up and down, whinnying. She couldn't take her eyes off the magnificent animal.

Forest noticed her interest. "You'll have to excuse Black Knight, he's a little…stirred up." Just then a high-pitched whinny came from the barn. "He's going to stand in stud today."

Cyndi didn't have to live on a ranch to know what that meant. "How nice for him."

Just then a man's loud voice came from inside the barn. Nora said, "Don't let Patrick's bark scare you off. He's a real sweetheart. C'mon." Nora went inside.

Patrick? Cynthia froze. No. It couldn't be the same man, she told herself.

Kelly nudged her down the cement aisle lined on either side with horse stalls, some empty, some with horses inside that came forward to welcome them. Cynthia could smell a sweet mixture of hay and horses in the immaculate barn.

At the far end a tall man stood with his back to them. Even before he turned around, Cynthia knew who he was. Oh, God. This had to be a bad dream. She quickly took in his blond hair partially covered by a white cowboy hat. It was the same face, the same chiseled jaw that she'd stroked so many times last night, and the same mouth that had done so many incredible things to her during their lovemaking. Finally she raised her gaze and looked into those blue, blue eyes.

Cynthia fought for a breath. She needed her best acting performance to get through this meeting.

Nora's voice broke through Cynthia's reverie. "Kelly, Cyndi, I'd like you to meet my brother, Patrick. Patrick, this is my boss, Kelly Reynolds, and her sister, the actress Cynthia Reynolds."

"Oh, my God," Kelly said. "You were at Morgan's last night. You were with—" She gave Cynthia a confused look, then quickly masked it as she turned back to Patrick.

Patrick nodded, fighting to act nonchalant. But too many emotions were churning through him, the most prevalent being anger. So his Cyndi was Cynthia Reynolds. And last night the famous actress had been looking for some entertainment. He'd just been a diversion to her.

"Yeah, I was at the pub. I was supposed to meet Nora, but it seemed she had a flat tire." He glanced at his sister. "If you want to show your friends around the ranch, it's not a problem, but I'm breeding the Keefers' mare this morning." He shot a hard look at Cynthia as he rubbed the mare's nose.

"She's beautiful," Cyndi said. "What's her name?"

Patrick had trouble listening to her soft, husky voice. "Suzy Q." His gaze bored into her startled brown eyes. "Now, if you'll excuse me…" He started to open the stall.

"Wait, Patrick," Nora called. "I need to talk with you." She took him by the arm and started off, but looked back toward Kelly and Cyndi. "Kelly, will you take Cyndi up to the house? I have coffee and Danish in the kitchen. I'll be up in a few minutes."

"Maybe we should just go," Cyndi said. "This wasn't a good idea."

"No, it's fine," Kelly said. "We'll be at the house. Nice to meet you, Patrick."

Patrick watched both women walk off. He wanted to run after Cyndi and demand to know why she hadn't told him who she was. But he first needed to speak with Nora. He had a feeling that she'd set something up. She usually didn't bring strangers to the ranch without telling him.

He folded his arms across his chest. "Okay, talk."

Nora forced a smile. "She's beautiful, isn't she?"

"Who?" As if he didn't know.

"Cynthia Reynolds, that's who." She rolled her eyes. "And she came here for help."

Now all the pieces were starting to fall together. "Was Cynthia the reason for our meeting at Morgan's last night?"

"Well, kind of." She wrinkled her nose. "I was hoping that if you met and liked each other, that you would want to help her."

Oh, brother. He'd helped her all right…and Cyndi had helped him, too. He drew a calming breath. "Just how am I supposed to do that?"

"She has this movie part coming up and it's a Western and…you need to teach her to ride."

Great. When did things get so bad that he had to teach a spoiled Hollywood actress to ride a horse? "Like hell. I don't have the time or the disposition to put up with a demanding actress." He couldn't stop the flood of memories of last night. Cyndi was demanding, all right, as a lover, but she had been just as giving. He turned away.

"Patrick, wait. You don't understand. She's terrified of horses."

"Not my problem."

"She's willing to pay twenty-five thousand dollars."

He stopped and stared at his sister. "You're kidding."

She shook her head. "I know you normally work with children, but Cyndi needs to be able to ride for this movie. When Kelly told me about it, naturally I thought of you. You are the best."

Patrick hated it when his baby sister pulled this sweet act. Ever since she was a kid, she'd brought home all kind of strays. He still had two dogs and a cat that she'd rescued. But this… "I have too much to do."

"I thought your dream was to enlarge the vineyard, to start a winery. Helping Cynthia Reynolds will bring you a lot closer to that goal."

It would take a long time for Patrick to save that kind of money. But the problem was, could he get past his relationship with Cyndi? Hell, what was he talking about? It was a one-night stand.

"Tell her I'll give her some time in the afternoon."

Nora looked funny. "Patrick, she needs more than that. You've got to work with her full-time. And this has to be a secret. That means she should live out here."

"So what exactly happened between the two of you last night?" Kelly asked curiously. "The man didn't seem to be too happy to see you. And before you deny it, I saw the sparks between you two, but I wasn't sure if he was going to throttle you or jump your bones."

Cynthia paced the large farm-style kitchen. Although the room had obviously new maple cabinets and the countertops were tiled in a natural-colored stone, there was a homeyness about the place that was warm and inviting. But no matter how inviting, she wanted to leave, to convince Kelly to take her back to town.

"I never told him who I was last night. We only exchanged first names." She tucked a wayward strand of hair behind her ear. "What's the big deal? You encouraged me to share a few drinks and some laughs."

Last night's memories were still fresh in her mind, still stirred feelings within Cynthia. She couldn't believe how much she'd wanted Patrick just hours ago. So much so she couldn't keep her hands off him. Seeing him again this morning, she realized those feelings hadn't gone away. Trying to work with Patrick Tanner would be a disaster.

"Are you saying that more happened between you two?" Kelly's eyes were wide with hope and surprise.

"Since when do we—" Just then the back door opened and Nora walked into the kitchen.

"Sorry to keep you waiting," she said. "Patrick and I needed to go over some things." She released a long breath and looked at Cynthia. "My brother wants to talk to you. He's outside on the porch."

"Look, Nora, if this is going to cause trouble…" Cynthia began.

"No, he just wants to make sure that you're serious about learning to ride. And to work out a few details."

Cynthia nodded. Good. She would straighten this out. She'd tell Patrick Tanner she didn't need his services and leave. There had to be dozens of instructors who could teach her to ride.

She walked out the door and found him sitting on the back-porch railing. His arms were folded over that gorgeous, broad chest. She shook away the mental picture of Patrick naked, then her gaze connected with his. "Look, Patrick, I'm sorry about last night."

"What are you sorry about, Cyndi? That you spent the night with me, or that your little joke backfired?"

"It wasn't a joke. You may not believe it, but I don't make a habit of going to bed with men I just met."

He didn't look like he believed her. "No problem. We used protection."

Seeing her pained look, Patrick wanted to take back his words.

"How come it's only my behavior that's being scrutinized?" she asked. "Is it because I left you first, instead of you leaving me?"

Her fiery question hit home.

He fought back. "How about because you didn't mention that you're Cynthia Reynolds? Was that the reason you wanted to leave it at just first names?"

"You ever think maybe my reason was that people act differently around me when they know who I am?" she asked. "You didn't recognize me. It was nice being myself for a change. You didn't seem to care who I was."

Hell, she'd had him so hot he couldn't remember his own name. "What do we do now?"

She shrugged. "I'll just tell Kelly and Nora we can't work things out. Although, I would appreciate it if you gave me the name of someone who can teach me to ride." She glanced around, not really looking at him.

He could direct her to a half-dozen people, but he doubted she would get results in such a short time. "Nora said you only had ten days and needed to keep this quiet. That if the media gets wind of you taking riding lessons, you could lose the opportunity for this movie."

"It's not your problem. Tell your sister thanks and tell my sister that I'll meet her in the car."

Before Cyndi could pass him, he reached out for her. Mistake. The hot sizzle from the connection was unbelievable. What he was about to do was another mistake. "I'll do it. But by my rules."

Cynthia didn't pull away, but she didn't back down either. "What are the rules?"

"We'll work from early morning until the afternoon. You'll also be responsible for the care of your horse. There will be no media around, and you'll move out here for the next ten days." And he asked for a larger amount of money for his services than she had originally offered just to see how far he could go. He expected her to tell him to go to hell.

"And what if I don't agree?"

"Then we say goodbye…this time." Inside he wasn't sure what he wanted her to do. He knew he didn't need this distraction, but he still wanted Cyndi. Maybe during the ten days she'd be here, he would get her out of his system.

Cynthia stepped back. "I have one condition of my own. We keep this arrangement strictly business. What happened last night will not happen again."

We'll see about that, Patrick thought. "Agreed. Strictly business." He shook her hand then released it before he broke his promise right here and now. "Talk with Nora and she'll show you where you'll be staying."

He started down the steps toward the barn, then turned. "I'll be busy most of the day, so you'll be fending for yourself. But tomorrow I expect to see you in the barn at 6:00 a.m. If you're not, I'll figure you've changed your mind."

"Oh, I'll be there," she tossed back, a challenging look on her beautiful face. "So be ready to live up to your reputation."

Three

 Four hours later, Cynthia and Kelly returned to the
Tanner Ranch from town. Cynthia had brought
back her car, along with two suitcases filled with
jeans, blouses and a couple of pairs of boots for her
stay.

 Nora greeted them, then took her to the ranch
house, recounting some of the history of the hun-
dred-year-old structure. The place had been re-
modeled, showing off shiny hardwood floors
throughout covered partly by taupe-colored rugs.
The large, overstuffed furniture in the main room

was done in earth tones and arranged around the stone fireplace and a large television.

"Years ago Patrick knocked out the wall between the dining room and living room," Nora explained. "He said he needed to keep an eye on all of us girls and this way it was easier."

"What about your parents?" Cynthia asked, surprised that Nora hadn't mentioned them.

Sadness flashed in the young girl's eyes. "They're dead. My mother passed away when I was about nine and my father a few years later."

"I'm sorry." Cynthia knew how it was to be without a father since her parents were divorced, but to lose both would be devastating.

"Thank you. It was tough at first," Nora explained, "but Jane, Karen and I had Patrick. He was the one who kept the family together, who worked around the clock to save our home. He'd just turned twenty-one when Dad died, and had been handling the ranch long before that."

Nora managed a shaky smile. "Will you listen to me go on. I'm sure you're not interested in our family history."

"Not so. I know what it's like to be without a parent. Kelly's and my father left us when I was ten." Of course it had been better than the nonstop fights, Cynthia remembered sadly.

Just then the back door opened and Patrick walked in carrying her two suitcases. Kelly followed behind him with a small duffel bag. His wary gaze was directed at her. He didn't say anything, but the meaning was clear. He wasn't happy she was here.

"I'm putting these in Janie's old room."

Kelly handed Cynthia the duffel. "Better go with Patrick and see your accommodations."

Cynthia reluctantly crossed the room to the wide oak staircase. On the second floor, there was no sign of Patrick Tanner so she continued down the hall, glancing into several of the bedrooms. Each one of them was neat and tidy, adorned with subtle homey touches. So unlike her modern hillside house in LA. Finally she found her host in a soft yellow room with an ivory chenille bedspread covering a canopy bed. Cynthia smiled. She would have given anything to have had a room like this growing up.

At the row of windows across the room Patrick pulled back the floral curtains, then raised the windows, letting in the sweet-smelling country breeze.

Patrick turned around, but he refused to look at Cyndi. What had he done to deserve this? He never brought women to the ranch—to his home. Not since Gwen. Damn. He hated thinking about how stupid he'd been back then. How much it had nearly cost him.

"The bathroom is across the hall," he instructed her. "Towels are in the cupboard. I don't have a full-time housekeeper, so you'll have to make your own bed and clean up after yourself."

"I can manage that."

Patrick stole another look and his breath caught in his chest. She was beautiful. Her face, her flawless skin, those expressive eyes. Memories of last night came flooding back. Cyndi's passion, her eagerness in their lovemaking…then her disappearance. It had never crossed his mind that she was the movie star Cynthia Reynolds.

"Good," he said, "because no one here has time to wait on you."

"Patrick, have I made you angry?"

Hell, yes. "No, I'm just busy. I have a mare in season."

"Please, don't let me keep you," she told him without any sarcasm in her tone. "I said I didn't want any special treatment, and I meant it."

Cynthia wondered if she would ever again see the Patrick she'd met at Morgan's. The man who had been so attentive, so loving. She realized she wanted to see that sexy smile of his again.

He gave her a sharp nod. "Sounds good to me,"

he said, but remained standing there with his hands on his hips. Those narrow hips attached to those long muscular legs. She let her gaze move upward over his flat stomach, to his broad chest and shoulders, unable to erase the memory of every alluring naked inch of this man.

Her pulse shot off, racing. Staying here for the next ten days was going to be torture. If this movie role wasn't so important, she wouldn't be here.

She picked up one of her suitcases and tossed it on the bed just as Nora and Kelly came in, nearly running into Patrick as he tried to get out the door.

Nora called to him, "Patrick, I'm cooking a tri-tip roast for dinner so be on time."

He mumbled something impossible to understand, then all they heard were footsteps on the stairs.

"Oh, Cyndi, I had another room picked out for you," Nora said as she glanced around. "I don't know why my brother put you here. We can move you."

"No, this is fine. I think we've disturbed Patrick enough for one day. I'm going to try and do exactly what he wants." She glanced at her sister. "And you, I'm not finished with you. You didn't even give me a chance to decide what I wanted to do. I'm not sure I can handle this."

Kelly didn't seem fazed as she helped unpack the clothes, putting things inside the dresser drawers. "If I'd waited, the movie role would have been gone before you decided to get near a horse again."

Cynthia took out her cosmetic bag along with her bottle of NoWait oil. She glanced at Nora. "Is she like this at the office? If so, I feel sorry for you."

Nora smiled. "I thought my sisters and I were the only ones who argued like this. I'm the baby so I have no sympathy for older sisters. I got bossed around by everyone."

"Yeah, but I bet you were spoiled, too," Cynthia said, glaring at Kelly. "Just remember all the mistakes are made on the oldest child."

"And I got all your hand-me-downs," Kelly tossed back.

Cynthia knew that Kelly wasn't just talking about clothes. During their teenage years they'd shared a few boyfriends, too. She surprised herself by saying, "Not anymore."

Kelly grinned. "I guess there are some things we need to put off-limits."

Cynthia wondered what had gotten into her. Had she gotten territorial over Patrick? She shook away the thought, knowing she needed to concentrate on her challenge of learning to ride.

But which one was going to give her the most trouble—the horse or the man?

After dinner, Patrick stood out on the back porch watching a light rain wash over the mountains. Billowy clouds clung to the peak, hiding the last of the day's sun. He loved this time. The end of a busy day, when his body felt a satisfied tiredness, which meant he'd accomplished a lot. And he had. If everything went as planned, the mare Black Knight had covered today would soon test pregnant.

Later that afternoon, he and Forest had ridden out to check fences and the herd. The cows and the new calves were doing fine. Then they went on to the west section to check the ten acres of rootstock vines they'd planted last spring. And finally he'd made it home in time to have a great dinner.

He liked having his sister home and he loved her cooking. With Nora working in Portland she hadn't been able to get out to the ranch much. That meant he was usually all alone. Not that he got lonely. He had plenty to keep him busy. And that was the way he liked it.

Old memories rushed into his head. Aside from his sisters it had been years since he'd shared his life with anyone. Not since Gwen had ripped out his heart and nearly bankrupted him. He'd wanted a wife, a second mother for the girls, especially someone to love. But she had played him for a fool.

Since then, Patrick had decided that he didn't need the hassle or heartache. After striking out with Gwen, he realized he wasn't cut out for relationships. So he kept any associations with women short, nothing serious, nothing permanent. And he'd let them know the score by the second date. But waking up this morning in the hotel room alone meant he'd never get the chance for that.

Now he needed to stop remembering his incredible night with Cynthia Reynolds. His body suddenly stirred to life and he cursed his weakness. How was he going to handle having this woman around, sharing his home…his life?

Just then the door opened and Cyndi, Kelly and Nora walked out onto the porch. Nora came up to him. "Patrick, Kelly and I are headed back to town, unless you need anything."

My solitary life back, Patrick thought as he shook his head. "I can't think of a thing." He leaned down so his sister could kiss him goodbye.

"Then I guess I'll be going." She looked him in the eye. "Behave yourself. I'll call you tomorrow."

Kelly and Cyndi hugged, then she and Nora

walked to their cars. Cyndi waved until they drove off, then turned to Patrick.

"Would you mind if I stayed out here for a while? I'm a little too restless to sleep."

Yeah, he knew the feeling. "It's a free country."

Cynthia leaned against the post and looked toward the barn. This wasn't going to be easy, especially since she couldn't seem to push aside the feelings this man churned up in her. "You own a beautiful piece of Oregon, Patrick."

"I know. Wouldn't live anywhere else."

Cynthia knew she should go up to her room, but the draw to him was magnetic. She couldn't stop the need she felt to rediscover this handsome man with the killer eyes, sexy grin and to-die-for mouth. She moved closer and could feel his heat, smell his fresh soap scent.

"Nora said you've lived here all your life."

He gave her a stiff nod. "True."

"That's nice," she said. "After my parents divorced, our mother moved us all to L.A." She remembered the endless crummy apartments in bad neighborhoods. As a twelve-year-old kid, she'd dreamed of a house and no money problems.

But Carol Reynolds hadn't been good at handling money, a job and kids. She was never meant to be without a man. If only she'd known how to pick the right ones. After two more bad marriages, her mother had wisely chosen to stay single. Why not? Her oldest daughter made sure she'd been taken care of. Cynthia had made a lot of money in her career, even if she never worked again.

"I was there once," Patrick's voice broke into her reverie. "Hated the place. Too many cars and people."

"That's true. I don't like to drive around on the freeways, either." She glanced toward the shadow of the mountains. "Like I said, you live in a great place."

"Well, it may be a great place but we start early in the morning. So you need to get to bed."

He started to move away, and something made her touch his arm to stop him.

"Please, not yet," she whispered, not willing to end it. "It's barely dark."

Cynthia's heart began to race when he gazed into her eyes. "You're right." His warm breath caressed her face. "It's not nearly dark enough. I can still see the fiery highlights in your hair." His gaze lowered. "And your sexy mouth."

The rush of pleasure his words caused was so intense she couldn't speak or resist when he reached for her and jerked her against him. Then he leaned down and took teasing bites from her lower lip. "Damn, you're too tempting."

She whimpered and her fingers gripped his shoulders.

His sapphire eyes met hers. "Want more?"

Cynthia's throaty whisper was barely audible, but he heard her. When he closed his mouth over hers, the muscles in her legs were suddenly nonexistent. But Patrick held on to her as his mouth moved over hers. His tongue slipped inside and rubbed against hers, recreating flashes of their night together. His touch, his mouth, his... Suddenly he released her and stepped back. His eyes were dark and intense.

"If you think this is going to make tomorrow easier, think again," he whispered. "So you better get some sleep." He turned and walked off the porch toward the barn.

Cynthia was still trying to catch her breath. What had gotten into her? What was it about this man that made her want her hands on him all the time? She'd never thrown herself at a man before. She raked her fingers through her hair. Well, she'd better think of a way to control herself and remember why she was here. To learn to ride.

She turned and headed inside the house. She doubted she'd be dreaming about horses tonight.

Patrick wasn't in a good mood the next morning. He'd been up by five to do chores, even though he hadn't slept much at all, not after kissing Cyndi. He'd lain awake, unable to get her out of his head.

He checked his watch. It was six o'clock and time to meet his student. He headed to the barn for the first lesson, but he doubted that Cynthia Reynolds was even out of bed yet. He groaned. The picture of the sexy redhead in tumbled sheets was not something he needed to think about. At least it meant that he could send her packing and out of his life. Then he could get back to normal.

Patrick walked into the barn and stopped when he saw his student standing in the center aisle. Dressed in worn jeans and a pink blouse, she looked too damn good for this early.

"Am I on time?" she asked.

"You're fine." He ignored her cheerfulness, trying to stay down to business. "Follow me," he said and walked to a stall. A camel-colored horse with a white star on her forehead immediately came to the gate. Cyndi stopped about ten feet back and her face turned pale.

Patrick frowned. "What happened to you?"

"What do you mean?"

"What's the reason you're so terrified of horses?"

She shrugged. "A horse is a big animal."

"Yeah." He petted the animal. "But something else happened to make you look like you're going to pass out. And if you want to ride, you better tell me what I'm dealing with."

Cyndi let out a breath. "When I was six, my dad took us to his family's farm in Missouri. He thought it was time that I learned to ride. All I can remember was that the horse was huge, but my dad still put me in the saddle. I begged him to take me off. He told me not to be a baby. The animal started moving sideways and I screamed when I lost control and ended up falling off. I broke my leg…and ruined the family vacation."

"I'd say your dad was a fool. Sounds like the horse wasn't used to kids." He went to the gate and rubbed the mare's nose. "Daisy isn't like that. She's the sweetest animal here. All my sisters learned to ride on her. Isn't that so, sweetie?" He crooned to the horse, but when he glanced at Cyndi she didn't looked convinced. "Look, I'm not going to force you to do anything. Maybe you're not ready to get on a horse today. The first step is to get used to your mount. So come here and just pet Daisy."

Surprisingly Cyndi did as he asked, came closer and reached out a shaky hand. Patrick took her sweaty palm and placed it against Daisy's forehead. The animal obviously welcomed the attention. "See, she likes it."

Cyndi smiled and Patrick felt it all the way to his toes as she continued the stroking.

"You're such a pretty horse," she said.

Daisy bobbed her head and they both laughed.

"I'd suggest you take this slow, but you only have ten days. Now, I have no idea what horses they'll be using in the movie, but if you learn what to *do* and what *not* to do around a horse, that should help you."

Cyndi nodded. "At this point, anything would help me."

"You have to know that animals sense your fear, but a little respect is a good thing. As you mentioned, horses are a lot bigger than we are. I've trained all the horses on the ranch and I've never raised a hand or a whip to any of them. I find they respond better to a gentle touch and my voice."

Cynthia already knew firsthand about Patrick's gentle touch. She blinked away the memory and turned back to Daisy. "I can do that."

"Good," he said, then smiled. "For the next ten days the two of you are going to spend a lot of time together. You'll be Daisy's sole caretaker. You'll not only be riding her, you'll feed her, groom her and clean her stall." His blue eyes locked with hers. "If you can't handle that, now is the time to let me know."

Cynthia knew he was giving her a chance to quit. Not to say she hadn't thought a lot about it during the night. She could walk away, go back to Hollywood and find another movie. No! She wanted this one. She wanted the role in *Cheyenne*.

"Show me what to do."

"First, you and Daisy need to get familiar with each other. She has to get used to your voice, your commands. You two need to become friends."

Cynthia followed Patrick to a room at the end of the barn. Inside, the scent of leather and polish was overwhelming but pleasant. She glanced around at the dozens of saddles atop sawhorses, and walls lined with bridles and halters.

"Later on you'll come in here to get Daisy's tack, so you're going to have to know where to put everything back where it belongs." He took a leather halter from a hook, then went to one of the saddles with beautiful hand tooling. "When the time comes, this will be the saddle you'll use. And you have to be strong enough to get it on Daisy."

She nodded, then followed Patrick back to Daisy's stall. He opened the gate and went inside. He ran his hand over the horse, speaking softly as he examined her, then slipped the harness on. "Watch how I'm doing this because tomorrow I'm going to expect you to be able to handle it."

"What if I can't?" she asked.

He stopped what he was doing and studied her a moment. "If I didn't think you could do this, I never would've considered taking you on."

"You're doing just fine," Patrick said as he watched Cyndi lead Daisy around the corral. He could see her uneasiness, but she was toughing it out and doing everything he'd asked of her. The old mare was a trouper, too. She could put up with nearly anything as long as she got some attention.

"Talk to her," Patrick coaxed. "Daisy will respond to your voice."

It was then he suddenly realized his mistake as he watched Daisy nudge her head against Cyndi's back, pushing her forward. Before Patrick could react, the horse had nudged her again. Cyndi kept moving away but the horse came after her.

"Patrick!"

He grabbed the reins. "Whoa, girl," he commanded the horse, then putting himself between Daisy and the frightened Cyndi, he calmed her. "It's okay, Cyn. She's just looking for her treat."

The redhead looked confused. "Treat?"

"An apple, a carrot. It's my fault." With Cyndi gripping his arm, he looked toward the barn. "Hey, Forest! Bring me a few apples from the bin."

Cyndi started to move away, but he held her against him. Damn, she felt good. "No, you're not going anywhere. Daisy may have gotten a little excited, but you need to learn to handle it. If you run away now, you're only feeding your fears."

Cyndi nodded. "Okay."

"That's my girl." He couldn't help but smile at her grit.

Just then the foreman came out with the apples and handed one to Cyndi. Forest grinned at her. "I take it Daisy let you know you forgot something."

Patrick held Daisy away from the treat. "Put an apple in your palm and hold it out to her."

Cyndi did as he asked and Daisy politely took what she offered. "I did it." She giggled as if she had done some incredible task.

Patrick found himself smiling again. He glanced over at Forest, who cocked an eyebrow, then walked away. "Just so you know, there is an apple bin in the barn," Patrick said. "So tomorrow bring one with you and you can give it to her." He rubbed the horse's nose and fed her the other apple. "Daisy's my special girl. After our parents died, we had to sell off most of the stock, but I managed to keep her." The horse bobbed her head up and down, knowing he was talking about her.

"I think she knows you love her," she spoke softly. "Thank you for letting me learn with her." She surprised him and began to stroke the horse, then took the reins from him. With a tug, she and Daisy started around the corral again, and all the while Cyndi spoke in a soft, soothing voice.

He released a frustrated breath. Her voice was anything but calming him.

An hour later Cynthia was busy doing the tasks that she would be expected to do during her stay at the Tanner Ranch.

Cynthia found she was a little disappointed that she wasn't going to get to ride today. Patrick had said that she needed to know her mount, so he'd tied Daisy to the post in the barn and showed her how to brush the horse.

She wiped the sweat from her face as she worked the currycomb over the horse's hindquarters, leaving a shine on the buckskin coat. All she knew was this was the best workout in the world.

She definitely could bypass her exercise routine tonight, but she wouldn't forget to apply her No-Wait oil. For the past two weeks she had religiously been applying the homeopathic oil behind each ear. She'd lost a few pounds, but mainly she had noticed she'd developed more muscle tone, a good thing since she was going to use those muscles while riding.

Forest walked by. "How are you doing?" he asked as he paused to talk with her.

She smiled at the friendly foreman with the warm hazel eyes. "Not too bad. Daisy and I are getting to know each other."

The horse continued to eat her oats from the feeding trough.

Forest ran a hand over the animal's rump and gave it a friendly pat. "Daisy's a good old girl. The kids love her."

Cynthia was confused. Was he talking about Patrick's sisters? "What kids?"

Before Forest could answer, she heard Patrick's voice. They both turned to see him, completely covered in mud from his face to his boots. "It's nice that all the chores are done so you can stand around and visit," he said.

"What the hell happened to you?" Forest asked, fighting laughter.

"Let's just say I tangled with a not-so-agreeable steer," Patrick grumbled. "I could have used your help out in the pen."

"Hey, you didn't ask."

Patrick glared at Cynthia, making her feel as though she was the problem. "Did you want me to help?" she asked.

"Sure. Think you can hold down a yearling calf so I can inoculate him?"

"I can try," she offered. She found she was curious about the workings of the ranch.

"That's all I need, for you to get kicked or worse. You better stay with Daisy." Patrick turned back to Forest. "I'll get the syringe and meet you out in the pen." He stalked off.

"Guess I'd better get back to work. Pat's irritated enough. I don't want to push him any further by talking with you."

"I didn't know I was off-limits."

Forest shook his head. "The next week is going to be interesting. See you later."

Cynthia went back to brushing the horse's camel-colored coat. "Oh, Daisy, will we ever understand why men act the way they do?" She brushed harder and the horse shifted sideways. "Sorry."

Once she'd learned that the man she'd spent the night with would be her riding instructor, she never should have agreed to stay here. Even though they'd said they would keep it business, she had already allowed Patrick to kiss her. And to tell the truth, she wanted to do a whole lot more than share a few kisses. That was her problem. Her desire for the man had her thinking X-rated thoughts. Her skin suddenly turned warm. Oh, yes, she was hot for the man. She continued to brush, hoping to distract the direction of her thoughts.

Around noon, a filthy dirty Cynthia walked to the house. She had groomed and fed her horse, and even worse, cleaned out the stall. She didn't care where Patrick had gone; all she knew was she needed a break.

In the bathroom she stripped off her clothes and took a quick shower, then came downstairs to start lunch. There were plenty of leftovers and she made herself a roast beef sandwich. Not forgetting about Patrick, she made him up a couple, and added two more to the stack for Forest. If they didn't show up, she could take them down to the barn.

Just then the two men walked through the back door. She noticed that Patrick had removed his soiled shirt, leaving his white T-shirt stretched across his broad chest. He stopped on seeing that she had fixed them lunch.

She set the table, then poured them all glasses of milk. She found a bag of chips and set it out.

"Hey, this is great," Forest said. "Thanks, Cyndi."

"You don't have to do this," Patrick finally spoke.

She shrugged. "It's not a big deal to make a few sandwiches." Both men went to the kitchen sink to wash up, while she pulled out a chair and sat down.

"Hey, I appreciate your effort," Forest said. "Peanut butter and jelly gets old."

"Well, you'll have to thank Nora. She's the one who made the roast last night."

Forest dried his hands on the towel and sat down at the table across from her. "Is she coming back tonight?"

Patrick pulled out a chair. "Nora does have a job."

Forest's gaze went to Cynthia. "I know. She works for your sister, Kelly. The lawyer. Right?"

She nodded, noticing his subtle interest. "Yes, she has a practice in Portland."

The foreman shook his head. "Beauty and brains, not to mention guts, all in the same family."

"Why do you say that?" she asked.

Forest took a drink of milk. "Because you both have demanding and successful careers."

She didn't want to go into her lack of movie roles the past few years. "I've been lucky."

He smiled and tiny lines appeared around his eyes. "Don't sell yourself short, Cyndi. Your talent has had a lot to do with it."

Before she could say anything, Patrick's chair scraped the floor as he got up. "It's time to get back to work." He carried his plate to the sink where he stood and finished his milk.

"Patrick," she called to him, "what do you want me to do?"

"Take the rest of the day off. I'm going to be busy." With those parting words, he was out the door.

Cynthia didn't know what to say. She looked at Forest. "What just happened here?"

"Nothing that's your fault. Patrick likes you well enough. He's just not sure he can trust you, but then he hasn't trusted any woman in a long time."

So the fascinating Patrick Tanner had a past—had been hurt. Cynthia couldn't help but wonder what kind of woman could walk away from this man.

Four

Two hours later, Patrick was still fuming. He pulled on his horse's reins to slow him, then started walking along the barbed-wire fence. He turned in the saddle and saw that Forest was in his sights.

What the hell was wrong with him? He didn't have any hold on Cynthia Reynolds. They'd spent one night together. She was only around now because she was paying him a lot of money to teach her to ride, not to give her attitude.

Patrick blew out a long breath. He'd prided

himself on his control. For years, he'd fought hard to be nothing like his father. Michael Tanner hadn't set much of an example for his son. He'd drunk to excess and used his fists freely, especially on his wife and kids. Years ago, the old man had told his son that a few slaps kept them in line. They needed to learn respect, just like his daddy had taught him.

Patrick was the second generation Tanner who'd been raised by an abusive father. Shutting his eyes, he felt his gut clench, remembering the awful circumstances of his mother's death. The police had called it an accident. He knew better. He didn't doubt that Mary Tanner had died at her husband's hands when he'd shoved her down the basement stairs. He took several calming breaths, but it didn't ease the guilt he'd carried with him for years. If he'd been home that night, he could have saved his mother.

Patrick heard Forest ride up.

"Hey, boss, you think I can have the night off if I get all my chores done?"

"Knock it off." Patrick didn't need his friend's sarcasm.

"Look, Pat, I'm not interested in Cyndi. She's nice and I like talking to her. That's all."

"Why should I care if you are?"

"Because, my friend, whether you want to admit it or not, *you're* interested in her. You can't even stand it when she talks to me."

"That's crazy." He knew it was a lie, but he wasn't going to admit to anything. "She's just a client I'm teaching to ride. Yeah, she's moved into my house and disrupted my life, but she's also paying me enough to help plant a lot more acres of vines next spring." He glanced at his friend and business partner. "That should make you happy since you're in this venture, too."

"I'll always be your friend first, whether we're in the wine business or not. You can tell me to stay out of it but something is going on between you and Cyndi."

"It's past tense. Something did happen between us, but that's over. This is business. All the money from Ms. Reynolds's riding lessons will be put into the vineyard."

Patrick had known Forest Rawlins for the past eight years. He'd come to the ranch looking for work right after the second-worst time in Patrick's life. Gwen had run off with nearly everything. It wasn't until later that he'd discovered that Forest had an MBA in business, but had gotten fed up with the corporate life. Forest had just picked up and walked away from everything. But when he came to the Tanner Ranch, he'd also brought enough knowledge to help Patrick save the place.

He resided in the small foreman's cottage and was paid a reasonable salary, and Forest claimed he'd never been so content. Now they were starting a partnership in the wine business. Patrick hoped in a few years they would be producing grapes.

"Let's go check our vines." Patrick kicked his horse's sides and rode off, refusing to answer any more questions.

As he rode along he tried to concentrate on the calming scenery: the rich green hues of the valley, the high blue sky, the bank of white clouds just hiding the tips of the Cascade Mountain Range. He walked Ace along the trail, through the giant pines, and felt a deep pride at being a part of this land. Tanner land. His chest tightened as he came to a clearing and looked down at the ten acres of row after perfect row of rootstock vines that he and Forest had planted last spring.

This was the beginning of his dream.

Cynthia wasn't going to sit around the rest of the day. After she put the plates and glasses into the dishwasher, she returned to the barn. Braver now, she went to check out the other Tanner Ranch residents and discovered she wasn't alone.

A tall, lanky teenage boy came out of one of the stalls carrying a bucket. "You must be Cyndi," he said.

"Yes, I am." Once again she was glad that she hadn't been recognized.

"You work here?" she asked. Patrick hadn't told her about any other employees.

"I'm Kevin Northbrook." He set the bucket down and tipped his hat, revealing short blond hair. "I help out some, mostly because it pays to board my horse. Patrick is cool. When my dad wanted to sell Ranger, Patrick said I could keep him here as long as I help out to pay for feed. So I come by as often as I can." He stepped back to the stall gate and a brown horse with a black mane came to him. "This is Ranger. Ranger, meet Cyndi."

The horse's head bobbed and Cynthia smiled. The boy held Ranger still while she petted him. The horse blew air out of his nostrils and Cyndi almost pulled away, but stood her ground.

Kevin smiled. "He likes you."

"I have to admit, I'm a little afraid of horses, but Patrick is helping me get through it."

"I know. He told me you were staying here for

a little while and I wasn't to tell anybody because you were up for a movie role and needed to know how to ride a horse."

Cynthia was a little surprised that Patrick would confide in this boy. "You know who I am?"

"Of course." He smiled. "Who wouldn't recognize Cynthia Reynolds? You've been in about a gazillion movies. My mom loves you."

She bit back a groan. Great! His mother loves me.

"It's nice to know that I have fans. But I'd appreciate it if you kept it quiet. I don't want the media discovering I'm here."

"Don't worry, it's cool. I can keep a secret. I haven't even told my mom or sisters. But could you sign an autograph for my mom before you leave?"

She smiled at the boy's thoughtfulness. "My pleasure. And I'd like you to help me."

His grin widened. "Sure, anything. I just have a few chores to do first."

"Maybe I can help you."

He studied her. "You'll get pretty dirty."

"You think I can't handle a little dirt? I guess you didn't see me in the movie *Romancing a Stranger* where I was in a fight and got shoved down a muddy hill." When Kevin shook his head, she continued. "It took us four takes to do it just right for the director."

"Wow, that's so cool. A lot better than mucking out stalls."

They started walking down the aisle toward the next stall. "You wouldn't say that if you had to do some of the things I've had to do in movies. I could tell you stories…."

It was about four o'clock when Patrick and Forest rode back to the barn. He hadn't planned on being gone all afternoon, but he needed time away from Cyndi. He wasn't used to having someone around, someone so disturbing. And she would be in his house, and in his life for the next week. Worse, every time they were together, he couldn't keep his hands off her. She wasn't doing much to resist him, either. He thought back to the kiss they'd shared on the porch. Of course that was tame compared to the wild night of passion just forty-eight hours ago.

Of course that wasn't an excuse to leave Cyndi to fend for herself. Oh hell, maybe he should just send her down to Gus Peters's place and let him deal with her. His neighbor would love the notoriety and before long would be holding a press conference for anyone who would listen.

Suddenly, Patrick's protective instincts kicked in. There might not be any future for the two of them, but that didn't mean he couldn't help her reach her goal. She was paying him a fortune just for the simple task of learning to ride. Besides, he was a grown man. If he couldn't control his urges, then he had a big problem.

"Hey, Pat, you have to see this," Forest called from the barn door leading to the corral. He walked over just in time to hear Cyndi's throaty laughter. Looking out to the arena, he saw her and Kevin along with the six-month-old bay colt, Spirit. They had the playful animal cornered and Kevin gave the cloth halter to her.

Slowly, Cyndi approached the horse, all the while speaking in a soft voice. The colt's ears perked up in interest and it froze as if mesmerized. A thrill of excitement rushed through Patrick as Cyndi continued to croon and walk toward the horse. With a slow hand, she slipped the halter over Spirit's face and Kevin buckled the strap. Then she took hold of the lead rope and the boy gave her a high five.

"Will you look at that," Forest said. "She's a natural with animals."

Patrick glared at his friend's satisfied look, then returned his attention to the pair working with the colt. There was deep concentration on Cyndi's face as Kevin instructed her on what to do.

"Maybe Kev should be her teacher," Patrick said.

It was Forest's turn to frown. "Sounds to me like you're running scared."

Maybe he was, but he wouldn't admit it. "I'm busy."

"For what she's paying, I'd never be that busy."

Patrick tensed. "You're not me."

"We've all been hurt, Pat, but you can't let the past affect your…opportunities. Cyndi seems like a nice person."

Forest had never spoken much about his own past, but he had been married years ago. And Patrick never asked for any details.

"Yeah, and she's so out of my league."

Forest snickered. "Yeah, aren't we all. But you might be surprised with Cyndi." Just then a car pulled up into the driveway, and Kelly Reynolds climbed out. "Speaking of opportunities…" Forest smiled. "I would never pass up a pretty blonde. Brains and beauty are a great combination." He pushed away from the fence. "I think I'll go greet our visitor."

Amazed, Patrick watched as Forest strolled off toward the expensive sedan and the attractive lawyer. The man had a slow, deliberate walk, taking his time to reach Kelly Reynolds. Forest had a way with people. He put them at ease with his friendliness, and by Kelly's reaction, she wasn't immune, either. Forest took her hand and after a few minutes he had her laughing. They were walking toward him when Patrick heard Kevin's warning yell. He turned back in time to see Cyndi sitting in the dirt holding her leg.

Patrick hopped the fence and was beside her immediately. "You okay?" Then before she could answer, he looked at Kevin. "What the hell happened?"

Cynthia couldn't believe it when she looked up and saw Patrick. "It's nothing," she said, her leg stinging. "Spirit and I were just getting to know each other and he got a little too playful and kicked me."

Kevin knelt down beside her. "I'm sorry, Cyndi. Spirit has a habit of playing a little rough."

"And if you knew that, why did you let Cyndi handle him? She's not used to being around horses."

Kevin's face flushed and Cynthia felt bad. "It was my fault, Patrick. Kevin warned me that Spirit kicked, but I got cocky."

Patrick wasn't paying attention to her explanation. He pushed up her pant leg, exposing her boot.

"See, my leg was protected by my boot." Her leg hurt some, but she was more embarrassed when she looked up and saw Kelly and Forest running across the corral.

She pushed Patrick's hands away from her leg. "I'm fine. Just help me up."

His blue eyes locked with hers. "I want to check you out."

She doubted he meant his words to sound so suggestive, but they did. She shook away the thought. "I'm capable of doing it myself. Just give me a hand up."

Finally Patrick stood and held out a hand. Cyndi was on her feet just as her sister got to her.

"Cyndi, what happened?"

"Nothing. I'm okay." She walked around, letting everyone see she was fine. Then she looked for Kevin and the colt, but they were gone. "Where is Kevin?"

"He's finishing his chores," Patrick said.

"But I want to talk to him." Cyndi started off toward the barn.

Her sister chased after her. "Cyndi, maybe you should go up to the house. Look at you. You're a mess." She wrinkled her nose. "And you smell."

Cynthia looked at her soiled jeans and blouse, recalling her working afternoon. "Oh, I guess I do."

"What have you been doing?"

Cynthia glanced over her shoulder at Patrick and Forest, who were following them. "Chores. You name it and I've probably done it. Now, if you'll excuse me, I need to see Kevin." Her gaze met Patrick's. "I'm going to let him know that he didn't do anything wrong."

"Are you trying to embarrass me?" Nora asked Patrick as she paced angrily in front of the desk. The knotty-pine-paneled office had been his sanctuary over the years. A place he could go to be alone, to organize his thoughts and have some peace from a houseful of females. The room had been off-limits, but his sisters had ignored that rule and had come in when they needed to talk with their big brother.

"Cynthia Reynolds is my boss's sister, not to mention an award-winning actress." Nora suddenly stopped. "I did this for you. I thought you'd be happy with the extra money to help with the vineyard."

Patrick was beginning to wonder if it was worth it. An hour ago, Kelly, Forest, Cyndi and Nora were at the Tanner kitchen table talking and laughing while eating Nora's chicken and rice. After Forest escorted Kelly to her car, she drove back to Portland. Cyndi had gone to her room. He'd come into his office for some quiet, but his sister had cornered him.

"Patrick, are you listening to me?"

"I'm listening. And no, I'm not trying to embarrass you."

"Then why weren't you with Cyndi today? She could have been hurt badly."

"I was with her this morning," he argued. "I just rode out to check on the herd. I didn't expect her to clean out stalls, bathe horses and train colts and fillies." He was still shocked that she'd done so much.

"What did you think she would do? Sit around and play spoiled starlet?"

He stood up. "How the hell should I know? Look, she knew from the start I had a ranch to run."

"Forest and Kevin can do most of the chores. Oh, Patrick, you said you would do this, and I've never known you to go back on your word."

She blinked as if she were going to cry. Damn. He hated when she pulled that.

"I told her you were the best," Nora continued. "Please, don't let me down."

Patrick stood, came around the desk and pulled his sister into his arms. "Hey, don't cry." He remembered holding his nine-year-old sister after their mother had died. He'd promised her then that he'd always be there for her. That she could count on him. He needed to do this for her. "I won't let you down, honey."

She raised her head. "Then you'll spend the day with Cyndi tomorrow? Help her ride Daisy?"

"Can I break for lunch?"

Nora smiled. "I expect you to. Half the time, I don't think you eat all day. I'm staying here tonight so at least you and Cyndi will have a good breakfast."

"Good." He kissed her nose. "I've missed your biscuits."

"Then find yourself a woman who can cook and I won't worry so much."

He didn't want to get into this old discussion tonight. "You find me a woman who can make biscuits as good as yours, and I'll consider it."

Nora's pretty blue eyes lit up as she held out her hand. "It's a deal."

There was a little bruise on her shin. Who would have thought such a small horse could pack such a wallop? It was a good thing she'd had on boots.

Cyndi sat on her bed. She'd showered and lathered her filthy body twice before she was presentable enough to go down to dinner.

Now, dressed in a cotton nightgown, she wasn't going to have any trouble sleeping, especially when she had to be up at dawn.

She'd nearly forgotten one thing. Cynthia went to the dresser and opened the bottle of NoWait and, as instructed, dabbed some behind each ear. After returning to the bed, she lay back on the pillow and pulled the lightweight blanket over her. A soft breeze was coming through the open window, cooling the room enough to be comfortable. Cynthia tried, but couldn't erase from her memory Patrick's panicked look when he'd found her on the ground. There was definite concern showing in his eyes.

So far she hadn't been able to forget the fact that just two nights ago he'd made love to her. She closed her eyes, feeling her body grow warm and achy as she recalled Patrick Tanner's skilled hands against her skin. She shifted restlessly against the cool sheets, but found no satisfaction.

Cynthia groaned in frustration. What was she doing? The man was off-limits. So she had to quit thinking of him, of their night together. It was one crazy night! Besides, just because Patrick Tanner had wanted her didn't mean that was a good thing.

He didn't seem to like her. The familiar loneliness washed over her as she thought about her life. Her acting career had filled it to a point, but… She shook away the regrets. She couldn't think about a relationship with a man right now. She had to concentrate on learning how to ride. And, she hoped, in a few months, she'd be in Wyoming, starring in a movie.

That made her smile and she reached for the bedside light, but paused when there was a knock on the door. Thinking it was Nora, Cynthia called out for her to come in. She was surprised when Patrick came into her room and walked straight to her bed.

"I wanted to check to see if your leg is okay."

She worked to control her breathing. "I told you earlier that I'm fine." She pulled back the blanket and exposed her bare leg, but before she could cover it, Patrick gripped her ankle.

His warm hand nearly made her gasp, but she wouldn't give him the satisfaction. "I want to see for myself." He sat down on the mattress and began to examine the bruise high on her calf above her boot. Cynthia closed her eyes, feeling her body run hot. Every cell was aware of this man. No doubt, she wanted him. Angry with herself for being so needy, she jerked away.

"I thought you said that your boot protected you."

"As you can see, I'm fine."

Seeing Cyndi's long, smooth legs didn't help Patrick. Damn, they went on forever. His gaze went to her face, to see her dark eyes large and liquid with desire. His body took notice, and he wanted nothing more than to climb in bed with her and further the examination.

"You feel you're ready to ride tomorrow?"

She blinked. "Yes."

He nodded. "Seems you've overcome a lot of your fear. Maybe it's time to see if you can handle being in the saddle."

She smiled and something tightened in his chest. "You're serious?"

"I'm serious. And after seeing you today, I realize you're serious, too."

She lost the smile. "When it's my career, I'm always serious."

Patrick had another sleepless night. He couldn't get Cyndi's sweet, citrusy scent or the feel of her smooth leg out of his head. He hadn't had a good night's sleep since he'd met the woman.

Showered and dressed, he came downstairs to another shock. He expected to see his sister alone, but Cyndi was with her. She was dressed in jeans and a green blouse, looking too good this early in the morning.

"Good morning, Patrick," Nora said, smiling.

"Morning, Nora. Cyndi." They were cooking. "What are you two up to?"

Nora gave him an innocent look. "I promised you breakfast, so I'm showing Cyndi how to make biscuits."

Patrick forced a smile. "That's nice." He went to the coffeemaker and poured himself a cup. Taking a long drink, he leaned against the counter to savor the wonderful flavor.

"Great coffee, sis."

"Thank Cyndi, she made it."

"Thank you, Cyndi," he said.

"You're welcome. I just added a cinnamon stick."

Nora picked up two plates filled with scrambled eggs and crisp bacon. "Come on, it's time to eat."

She set the plates on the table as Cyndi pulled a sheet of biscuits out of the oven. Placing them in a basket, she brought them to the table and sat down.

"Well, it looks like my work here is finished." Nora pulled off her apron and laid it on the counter. "I'm headed back to town."

"Aren't you going to stay and eat?" Patrick asked.

"I ate while I cooked. Kelly needs me to come in early this morning. She'll be in court." She picked up her purse and headed to the door, then turned to Cyndi. "If he causes you any trouble today, just give me a call."

"Hey, you two, I'm right here," he announced, then took a bite of egg.

"I think I can handle him," Cyndi said.

Nora smiled. "I believe you can." Then she looked at her brother. "I'll see you tomorrow afternoon about two."

She waved and was out the door.

Patrick decided the only way he was going to survive the next week was to keep his hands to himself and his mouth shut. He continued to eat, then picked up a biscuit and buttered it, and took a bite. The flaky roll melted in his mouth.

"You really made these?"

Cyndi nodded. "Yes, I made them. Why are you so surprised?"

So many things about this woman surprised him. So far she hadn't demanded or complained about anything. And he'd dumped a lot on her trying to make her give up and leave.

He glanced across the table. Cyndi was beautiful, even devoid of makeup, with freckles dusting her nose and her long hair braided down her back. Her hands were nicely shaped, her fingers long, the nails cut short and with clear polish. Her toes were a different story, he thought, recalling the hot red color he'd seen last night.

And this morning, she'd made great-tasting coffee and flaky biscuits. Damn, he was in big trouble. He was doing everything in his power to stay away from her. He'd actually made it through yesterday without kissing her. And now his attention went to her inviting mouth and he started to salivate.

He had to get out of there. His chair scraped the floor as he stood and carried his plate to the sink, eating on the way. He came back to the table and grabbed two more biscuits and some bacon.

"I need to get some chores done before we start. I'll need about thirty minutes. Just leave the dishes. I'll get to them later." He rushed out the door, knowing he was the biggest coward in the world. But running was his only protection.

Later, Cynthia walked toward the barn, wondering if she was ready for this. Playing with the colt yesterday was a lot different than climbing onto a full-size horse. Even as sweet as Daisy was, she was fifteen hands high and outweighed her by nearly a thousand pounds. Then there was the fact that she'd be with Patrick Tanner all day. A man who aroused her whenever he got close.

Cynthia walked into the barn in time to see Patrick lift a large bale of straw off a wagon. He'd removed his shirt, revealing the straining muscles across his broad chest and huge arms. Beads of perspiration dotted his face and neck, causing his bare skin to glisten.

Oh, my! She tried to pull air into her lungs. Her gaze remained glued to his well-toned body, with his low-riding jeans revealing the dark blond swirl of hair that disappeared under his belt buckle. Memories flooded back of their night together. She'd known every glorious inch of this man. She knew from memory that he was total perfection.

Patrick looked up from his job and spotted her. "Hey, you're early."

"I finished in the kitchen. I—I can wait if you're busy."

He shook his head as he pulled off his gloves and wiped the sweat from his forehead. "Why don't you go and get Daisy's tack? I'll show you how to saddle her."

The cool tack room didn't do much to help Cynthia's condition. It had to be hormones, she thought. No man had ever affected her this way. She took down the bridle and tried to concentrate on Patrick's instructions. She wanted so badly to do well today. She carried the tack back to Daisy's stall, then returned for the saddle. By then Patrick was finished and buttoning his shirt.

"I could saddle Daisy for you," he began, "but it's important that you learn. And if someone else saddles your horse, it's always best if you double-check the cinches. It's your butt that lands on the ground if someone doesn't do his job."

First Patrick instructed her how to put on the bridle, then had her lead Daisy out of the stall and tie her to the post. Next Cynthia put on the blanket, then she lifted the saddle, and on the second try, she had it on Daisy's back. After Patrick showed her how to do the cinches and adjust the stirrups, she led Daisy out into the corral.

"Now hold the reins," he said. "Then grab hold of the horn, put your foot into the stirrup and pull yourself up."

Cynthia went to Daisy. She blew out a breath to relax. Her heart raced, but that was normal because of her excitement. Excitement, she told herself, not fear. She grabbed hold of the saddle horn and slipped her foot into the stirrup. Daisy shifted a little away from her. That was when she felt Patrick come up behind her to calm the horse.

"Whoa," he soothed Daisy. Then his large, sure hands went to Cynthia's waist, and awareness shot through her, making it nearly impossible to think about getting on a horse. It was a good thing he knew what to do and boosted her up.

"Swing your leg over," he told her and she did.

Cynthia held on to the horn as she shifted in her seat. She looked down at Patrick and smiled. "Hey, I made it."

"I can see that. How do you feel?"

She sighed. "Okay." She patted Daisy on the neck. "What about you, girl? Think you can take me for a ride?"

"Now, don't get too cocky," Patrick warned. "You have to crawl before you can walk. So you're going around the corral to start out." He went over the different commands, then sent her on her way. He watched her as she circled the arena. "Sit upright, but relax your shoulders. That's it. Relax your wrists. Now let go of the saddle horn."

"There is so much to remember." She felt herself tense.

Just then Patrick came up to the walking horse, grabbed the horn and pulled himself up behind her. "What are you doing?" she gasped.

"Just giving you a little help. If you want to get that part in the movie it would help if you look like you know what you're doing." His hands were on her shoulders. "Relax." He ran his hands down her arms, causing her to shiver. "Just let them hang loose. And hold your head up. Don't look down at the ground or at the horse's neck. It's kind of like dancing. You don't look at your feet."

Cynthia tried to listen to what he was saying, but with his body pressed against hers, his warm breath against her ear, all she could do was nod. Riding a horse was the last thing on her mind. She wanted to lean back into Patrick's body, have his hands journey over her....

His voice broke through her reverie. "You got that?"

Cynthia was jolted back to reality and nodded again.

He slid off the horse's rump just as smoothly as he got on.

"You ever thought about doing stunt work? You do that so well."

He smiled. "So do you. You look pretty good up there."

"I feel good up here. Show me more." She would like him back behind her, but maybe that wasn't a good idea. Not if she was to concentrate on her riding.

"Okay, if you're ready to turn, then gently tug the reins to the right or left."

Cynthia did as instructed, surprised at how easily Daisy followed her commands. This was good. Deciding to let this man teach her how to ride was the right way to go.

"Daisy is wonderful."

Patrick stood in the middle of the arena watching her closely. "Yes, Daisy's a sweet girl." The horse's ears pricked up when she heard her name.

"You just have a way with women."

She got a sexy grin from Patrick. "Tell me more."

Five

At ten that morning, Carrie Martin took one of the last seats in the back of the Healthy Living Clinic auditorium. The large crowd was buzzing with excitement as it waited for Dr. Richard Strong to start the seminar. Even though she knew that Richie wouldn't recognize her if she stood in front of him, her heart was pounding with anticipation.

Carrie's appearance had drastically changed over the years. There was nothing left of that shy, insecure girl he'd once known. She was proud of her new looks, her trim, curvy body. She'd gotten a new hairstyle and added highlights, even changed her eye color to a dazzling blue with contacts. No, she wasn't the same woman Richie had left in Florida all those years ago. She was educated and had a career she loved—teaching. She'd married again to her sweet late husband Ralph, but best of all, she had a wonderful son, Jason.

Suddenly Dr. Richie walked out onto the stage and the audience erupted in applause. Carrie sat up straighter to get a better look at the latest fitness guru. He was dressed in a charcoal custom-tailored suit, snowy-white shirt and a subtle deep maroon tie. His silver-streaked dark hair was styled to perfection. His magnetic personality showed as he walked to the front row and shook hands.

Carrie felt the tightness around her heart and quickly pushed back the feeling. She had to keep emotions out of this. Richard Strong had a lot to answer for. Twenty years, to be exact. She might not deserve any explanation, but their son did.

Even over the cheers, she could hear the ringing of her cell phone. She quickly pulled it from her bag as she climbed over people to leave the room. Once in the hall she hurried to a quiet corner and pushed the button.

"Hello," she answered, knowing it could only

be either her son or the restaurant, La Grenouille Dorée, where she'd worked as a hostess since coming to Portland.

"Mom," Jason spoke.

Carrie put her hand over her other ear so she could hear. "Jason, is something wrong?"

"That's what I was about to ask you. Mom, I wish you'd come home."

Carrie smiled sadly, hearing the worry in her son's voice. He'd gone though so much during his nineteen years.

"Jason, we talked about this before. It's something I need to do."

She heard his long sigh. "If you're doing this for me, don't. I don't need another father."

Cynthia was so in tune with her mission of trotting Daisy around the corral, she hadn't realized that the morning was gone. She'd been in the saddle most of it, and doing a pretty good job with the mare.

"I think you need to take a break," Patrick suggested while she continued around the arena.

"Not yet." She couldn't hide the disappointment in her voice.

She had worked through each and every command until the horse responded to her with ease.

And she was far past walking the horse. She could trot now.

"I'm just getting it right." There was so much to remember. She could feel the muscles in her legs tightening, and her arms were tired. She wasn't used to this kind of exercise, but she loved it. And she found she loved riding. Who would have thought it?

In the center of the corral, Patrick rested his hands on his hips. "If you don't stop, you'll be so sore you won't be able to sit in the saddle tomorrow."

Hearing his warning, Cynthia pulled back on Daisy's reins until she stopped. Patrick came over to help her dismount.

"I can do it," she said.

He nodded. "If you say so."

Cynthia slipped her right foot out of the stirrup and swung it over the back of the horse. She released the other boot and began to slide off Daisy. Suddenly the ground seemed a long way off and when she finally landed, whatever strength was left in her legs suddenly gave out.

Patrick grabbed her around the waist and held her up as she started to sway. He pulled her against him so she wouldn't crumble into the dirt.

"I told you, you overworked this morning," he said against her ear.

"I guess I am a little tired," she admitted, much too aware of his large hands on her.

His eyes grew dark. "Do you think you can stand on your own?"

"I guess there's only one way to find out." And she slipped out of his hold.

"I want you to rest this afternoon," he told her.

Regretfully, she moved away. Her legs were a little shaky, but she wasn't about to admit it. "I don't feel too bad. After some lunch and a couple of ibuprofen, I'll be ready for the afternoon."

"You can't do it all in one day, Cyndi. Your body isn't used to riding, and that bottom of yours is going to be sore as it is. So go up to the house and take a long soak in the tub, then rest. I'll take care of Daisy."

He started off with her horse, but she went after him. "I know what my body can and can not do, and I want to ride this afternoon."

Irritation flashed across his face. "You don't always get your way, Ms. Reynolds. Not around here anyway. You may want to ride, but I won't be there to help you. As I told you before, I have a ranch to run. We'll continue instruction tomorrow morning." His stern gaze held hers a moment, then he turned and led Daisy to the barn.

Cynthia kicked at some loose dirt. Who did he

think he was, telling her she couldn't ride? Well, she wasn't going to let him get away with ditching her again. She worked hard not to limp as she made her way toward the house. She would be back, just as soon as she rested.

The long, hot bath had done nothing to ease her anger. She stepped into a pair of sweatpants and groaned, feeling her sore, tired muscles less tense, but still painful. After pulling on a shirt, she wiped the moisture off the mirror, then brushed her damp hair into a ponytail. She then added moisturizer to her face, gloss to her dry lips, and noticed that her nose was sunburned.

No wonder Patrick had sent her away. She thought back to her lesson and how he'd stood in the corral, directing, encouraging her all morning. He never took a break, drank only an occasional bottle of water, and he'd been in the sun as long as she had.

So what had happened? Why did she feel as if she'd been dismissed and sent up to her room?

"Well, I can't waste time trying to figure you out, Mr. Tanner. If I can't ride, I have plenty of other things to do."

Cynthia gathered her dirty clothes and returned to her room. First thing, she picked up her cell phone and made a call to her agent to find out the status of the movie. She got good news. The director of *Cheyenne* was interested in having her read for the female lead. Cynthia needed to be back in L.A. in a week to audition for the part.

With renewed energy, Cynthia turned on the portable cassette player and started Dr. Richie's exercise routine. She knew the director was going to be looking at more than just her riding and acting ability. She had to look good in jeans, too.

Halfway through her high kicks, there was a knock on the door. Breathing hard, Cynthia went to see who it was, hoping Patrick was on the other side so she could slam the door in his face. But it was Nora, dressed in jeans and a T-shirt that read Tanner Ranch.

"Nora, I didn't know you'd be here. Do you need help with dinner?"

She shook her head. "I'm sorry to disturb you, but we need your help with something else. In ten minutes we're going to be invaded by about a dozen kids."

"Oh, really?"

"Twice a month Patrick and I work with boys and girls from a shelter in Portland. They've had it pretty rough and they really need this time with the horses. I hate to ask, but how do you feel about helping out? It'd be just putting them on horses and walking them around the corral."

"Sounds like something I can handle," Cynthia said, realizing now why Patrick couldn't spend time with her this afternoon. "I'll be down as soon as I can."

"I knew I could count on you." Nora smiled, then handed her a T-shirt. "Now you're official."

By two o'clock, Patrick had just finished a quick sandwich as the shelter's bus drove through the gate and stopped in front of the barn. Happy voices filled the air as the kids filed off. His attention stayed glued to each child who'd made it out today. Many of them had been coming here for almost a year, ever since Nora had suggested he start the riding program.

It was the best thing he'd ever done, bringing a dozen kids from the shelter out here twice a month. They came from abusive homes and were living in a children's shelter because there wasn't any room in foster care. He wished they could come more often, but with just himself, Nora and Forest, he couldn't handle any more.

"Is he here?" Nora asked.

Patrick glanced at his sister as she appeared beside him. He knew she was wondering if Davy Cooke was coming back today.

It had been last spring when the seven-year-old boy had stepped off the bus for the first time. Dozens of bruises were still evident on his small body from his mother and her boyfriend having used him as a punching bag. Patrick had trouble controlling his anger, ready to deal out his own brand of vengeance to the adults responsible. It had been the shelter counselor who'd told him how to handle Davy with kindness and love. That hadn't been easy, either.

At first, Davy had been angry and unresponsive, but when he came around the horses, things began to change. Still, Davy's biggest problem was that he challenged the rules, and as a result, he lost privileges. A visit to the ranch was a privilege.

He hadn't been allowed to come to the ranch for a month.

A curly-haired blond boy stepped off the bus. He was in jeans that were too big and a faded T-shirt, but his wide smile erased the shabby look. The boy ran up to Patrick.

"Hi, Patrick. Hi, Nora. I got to come back." Big brown eyes accented his freckled face.

"I can see that," Patrick said. He gripped the boy by the shoulders. "So I take it you're going to behave today," he said in a stern voice.

Davy glanced over his shoulder at one of the

counselors. "I will," he promised. "Do I get to ride Daisy?"

Patrick knew the boy loved the seasoned mare. Maybe too much. He also knew how healing an animal could be for a kid, especially when it was all he had. Daisy had given a lot of love to kids.

"You're in luck today, Davy, because that's who I gave you."

Cynthia came out of the house ten minutes later, eager to help. She saw the group of kids standing by the corral fence. Their age looked to be between seven and twelve years old. The high pitch of their voices told her of their excitement.

A cute little boy came up to her. "Who are you?"

"I'm Cyndi. I'm staying here for a while. What's your name?"

"I'm Davy. I'm going to ride Daisy."

She smiled. "You're pretty lucky, she's a nice horse."

"She's my favorite." Davy smiled, revealing a gap in front of his mouth where a tooth had been. The boy studied her with questioning eyes. "Are you going to help us ride, 'cause we hafta have adult superbision."

"Well, in that case, I guess I'd better help out."

Cynthia looked toward the corral to see Nora leading two horses out of the barn.

"Cyndi, will you go and saddle Daisy?" She smiled down at the boy. "For Davy."

"See, I told ya," the boy cheered.

"Okay, you stay right here and I'll be back as soon as I can."

It took Cynthia a little longer than usual because she wanted to double-check the tack. Then she led Daisy out to the corral where she found Patrick and Forest at the far end on a high wooden platform, helping one of the boys onto a horse.

The children wore helmets and stood in a line patiently, waiting for their turn on one of the six mounts.

Kevin came out of the barn, leading Ranger. He smiled. "So Patrick roped you into volunteering."

"Actually it was Nora. But I'm happy to help." She tugged Daisy in behind another horse, waiting to get to the stand and Davy. Patrick walked up beside her. His hat was cocked low on his head, and he was wearing a Tanner Ranch T-shirt the same as she had on. It just happened to look so fine covering his muscular chest and wide shoulders.

His voice drew her back. "Think you can handle a seven-year-old?"

She nodded, knowing that he was entrusting her with a big responsibility. "That is, if you just want me to walk Daisy around the corral."

He finally smiled. "Just don't let Davy talk you into anything more."

"I can handle him."

He gave her the once-over, causing her pulse to race. "No doubt." He tugged on Daisy's reins to bring the horse to the stand where Davy was waiting.

"Hi, Daisy," the boy said as he petted the horse's forehead. "I get to ride you." The mare bobbed her head, making Davy giggle.

Patrick helped the boy climb into the saddle, then he buckled the safety strap and sent them off.

Both Forest and Nora were leading two horses with young children. They were all moving lazily around the corral. Kevin had an older boy named Mike on Ranger, teaching him the different commands.

"Go faster, Cyndi. I want to go faster." Davy started kicking the horse's sides, causing Daisy to pick up her pace. Cynthia quickly took charge and pulled back on the reins.

"No, you don't, young man. We can't go fast because I can't go fast."

"But Patrick can make his horse go real fast."

"I'm not Patrick. I'm just learning to ride like you are."

"You are? How's come?"

"Because I wanted to learn." She patted Daisy's neck. "It's fun."

"Patrick says when us kids get really good he'll take us on a trail ride." He took a hand off the saddle horn and pointed toward the mountain range. "Up there. We're going to build a campfire. Just like real cowboys. And I get to wear a cowboy hat and boots."

Cynthia eyed the discount-store sneakers the child wore, and it tore at her heart. Never again would she complain about anything.

"Maybe if you ask Patrick, you can go with us."

Cynthia couldn't help but watch Patrick Tanner lift a little girl into the saddle. His face split into a wide grin and the girl smiled back. She could almost picture him doing the same thing with his own sisters.

"We'll see." She realized that she would like to go on a trail ride with them. She hadn't been around kids much, and she saw today what she'd been missing. They looked at her with such awe, such wonder. Would she have felt like this if she'd become a teacher?

"Are you anyone's mom?"

A familiar ache tightened in her chest at Davy's question. "No, I don't have any children."

She thought back ten years to her one long-term relationship with Clark Madison. He'd wanted to get married. At the time she'd been twenty-five, and her movie career was at its peak. She'd thought they had plenty of time. But they hadn't. Soon after that they broke up. The last she'd heard, Clark was married with three kids.

"My mom didn't want me." The words came out of Davy's mouth as if he had resigned himself to that fact.

She didn't know what to say. When those chocolate eyes lowered to hers, she wanted to pull him down from the saddle and hold him, comfort him. She swallowed hard, then turned away to see Patrick waving for her to bring Daisy over.

"Looks like we have to go back." She tugged on the mare's reins and led her to the stand where Patrick was ready to take Davy off.

The boy gripped the saddle horn. "I don't want to get off."

Patrick hesitated, but remained stern. "We've talked about this, Davy. Other kids need a turn." He reached for the child, but Davy pulled back. Cynthia hurried around the platform.

"Hey, Davy, why don't you come with me? I'll show you Daisy's stall." She gave a sideways glance at Patrick and saw that he wasn't happy about her stepping in. "We'll make sure that it's all clean for her when she goes to sleep tonight."

The boy brightened. "'kay." He gave Patrick a winning look.

Cynthia helped him from the saddle. "I'll watch him."

"You'd better," Patrick warned. "Don't let him talk you out of anything."

Cynthia wouldn't believe that a small child could be such a handful, but Davy certainly was. He asked question after question, and insisted on knowing about anything and everything, Patrick being his favorite topic. No doubt a lot of hero worship there.

"Sometimes Patrick gets mad at me, but he never yells or hits me." The boy sat on a bale of straw just outside the stall while Cyndi did the cleaning. She lifted the pitchfork and dumped the contents into the wheelbarrow.

"Even if I do bad things, he doesn't hit me," Davy said.

"That's because he's a nice man."

"He doesn't have any kids, either. Like you."

The boy lowered his head as he twisted a piece of straw. "I wish I could live here."

"It's pretty," she agreed. "I wouldn't mind staying here all the time, too. But we can't always have what we want."

"That's what Nancy says. She's my counselor." He smiled. "She took me away from my house." Those big brown eyes bored into hers. "I can't see my mom anymore. She was bad and went to jail."

Cynthia put her pitchfork down and sat beside the boy. "I'm sorry, Davy." She hugged him close, feeling tears gather in her eyes.

He finally pulled away, then climbed off the bale and carried some handfuls of fresh straw into the empty stall. "If I lived here, I would work all the time and take care of the horses, and I'd never say another bad word ever."

Cynthia fought a smile. "Do you say bad words?"

"Sometimes when I get really, really mad." He looked at Cyndi. "I didn't say any today."

Cynthia stood and caught sight of something out of the corner of her eye. Patrick was leaning against the next stall. His expression didn't tell her how much he'd heard.

He walked over to them. "Hey, Davy. Everyone is up at the house. Nora made some cookies."

The boy's eyes widened. "Peanut butter?"

"Peanut butter," Patrick agreed.

"Oh, boy," he said and took off running toward the house.

Cynthia looked at Patrick. "He's a great kid."

"You've only seen him on a good day."

"After the life he's had, I can understand why he's angry."

Something flashed in Patrick's gaze. "Life isn't perfect for a lot of kids. Davy's had it worse than most, but he's in good hands now."

"I know." She came out of the stall. "You act real tough, but you're a good man, Patrick Tanner." She started toward him. She couldn't seem to stop herself as she reached up and placed a light kiss on his lips. Before she could get away, he grabbed her and pulled her against him.

"You better be careful. A man could get the wrong idea."

Oh, she wanted him to get the wrong idea, but knew it would only make matters worse between them. "I'll try to restrain myself." With the last of her willpower, she pulled back from his embrace and walked out of the barn. She had to get away from this man…and soon.

That evening, Cynthia decided she deserved a treat, so she headed for the swimming pool at the clinic. She loved their water aerobics class. It was the best workout and she stayed clean. After changing into her street clothes, she was headed to Dr. Richie's seven o'clock seminar. She hoped to see Kelly there, too. Her sister didn't think much of the doctor's weight-loss plan, but went along. Cynthia liked being here because everyone was so positive and friendly, and after three days with Patrick Tanner, she needed her self-esteem boosted.

It was Dr. Richie who greeted her as she came into the auditorium. "Ms. Reynolds," he called to her.

Cynthia usually hated being recognized, but Dr. Richie was different. His books and tapes had helped her be more comfortable with who she was. And in this clinic, she felt safe from judgmental people.

She greeted him with a smile. "It's good to see you, Doctor."

Daniel O'Callahan watched the two from across the hospital atrium. He couldn't believe it was the beautiful actress Cynthia Reynolds. Wait until he told his grandmother. Maybe he could get an autograph.

He moved across the room just as the couple exchanged a handshake. The distinguished, gray-haired gentleman said goodbye.

"Goodbye, Dr. Richie," Cynthia Reynolds said with a smile. Then she turned to Daniel. "Hello."

He nearly swallowed his tongue. "Hi. I hate to bother you, Ms. Reynolds, but my grandmother is a patient here in the hospital and she loves all your movies. If it's not too much trouble, do you think I could get an autograph?"

"Of course. It's no trouble at all," she said. She took a notepad from the table and scrabbled on it. "I hope she feels better soon."

"I'm sure this will help."

She smiled again and walked away. He followed her departure, a little surprised over her friendliness. A lot of movie stars avoided people. He glanced around the hospital waiting area, noticing that since he'd been spending a lot of time at Portland General for his grandmother, he'd been noticing that most everyone had been friendly. And not just to him, but to each other. Not just friendly hugs, either, but continuous touching and kissing. He'd noticed several other couples in the halls acting the same way.

Was something going on, or was it just the cop in him that made him suspicious?

Six

Where the hell had Cyndi gone?

Patrick paced his bedroom. The large room had once belonged to his parents, but for the past ten years, and after an extensive remodeling, he'd claimed it as his.

The walls were a golden tan and the woodwork trimmed in an off-white. The honey hardwood floors were bare except for a scattering of plush area rugs. His king-size bed was covered with a navy comforter and deep green pillows. A connecting bath gave him all the privacy he'd once needed in a houseful of women.

What once had been his private retreat now was anything but, since Cynthia Reynolds had invaded his home…his life.

And yet, he had no claim on her…so why should he let the fact that she'd gone into town bother him? If she wanted to find male companionship, he couldn't stop her. He sure as hell didn't have time to play games, to cater to her needs.

Cyndi was only a resource to help him get closer to his dream. She was paying him generously to teach her to ride a horse. Nothing else. Just because they'd spent one night together didn't mean that he had any say about her actions.

Damn. He hated that she could stir him up like this. He glanced at the clock. It was after eleven and he suddenly realized there might be a totally different scenario. What if she'd been in an accident, or worse, and needed help?

He hurried from the room and down the stairs, then into the kitchen. Suddenly the door opened and Cyndi walked in.

"Where the hell have you been?" His gaze roamed over her, relieved that she was okay.

She gasped. "Patrick. You scared me."

"Where have you been?" he repeated.

"I was in town."

"Don't you think you're trying to squeeze in a lot of activity even for you?" Had she been with a man?

She placed her purse on the counter. "What are you talking about?"

"Look, I'm not going to waste my time with you if you're not serious. If you're going to be out all night drinking and picking up men—"

"Just stop right there," she interrupted. "For one thing, I've done everything you've asked of me."

"How do you know? You weren't here tonight," he yelled, trying to control his anger. It wasn't working. "I didn't know where you'd gone. The next time you decide to go man-chasing, let me know." His hands clenched into fists. He couldn't remember ever being this angry. It frightened him, and worse, he could see the fear in Cyndi's eyes.

He had to get out of there. Without a word he rushed out of the house and literally ran toward the barn. Once inside, he paced around as if he were a caged animal.

Patrick wanted to hit something. Anything. Suddenly, images of his father's drunken rages flashed in his head. Oh, God, his worst fears had come true. He'd turned into his old man. He marched back and forth along the aisle. Several of the boarded horses came to their stall doors, expecting some attention, but he ignored them.

He finally sat down on a hay bale and dropped his head into his shaky hands.

That was how Cynthia found him when she walked into the barn. She was a little shaky herself, but she wasn't about to let Patrick walk away from her like this. The things he'd said had hurt her.

"Did you really think I was out picking up a man tonight?" She watched his back tense as she approached him. "And what business is it of yours if I had?"

He finally looked up. "Does it matter?"

"Yes. You seem to think that I make a habit of finding men. Well, I don't." She closed her eyes, wondering why she cared what he thought. But she did. "I hadn't been with a man for over two years when I met you at Morgan's Pub."

He gave her a doubtful look, and it hurt.

She was angry now. "Why is it that men are never questioned when they take a woman to bed, but when women do it, they get reputations?" She studied him, finding she didn't want him to think the worst of her. "I have no idea why I came up to you at the bar. But in the end, you wanted me just as badly as I wanted you that night."

Patrick couldn't deny it and he hated that she'd gotten to him. "This isn't working, Cyndi. You make me feel…do things… I liked my life just as it was."

"I liked my life, too. I told you that my career is my life. I still need to learn to ride. Now more than ever, since I talked with my agent today. I have an audition in a week."

Her career was everything. Patrick needed to remember who she was. An actress. And a good one. "Maybe it would be best if Forest takes over."

"No! The deal was that you teach me. You're the best."

Patrick raked his fingers through his hair, trying to control his frustration. "You don't know, Cyndi. This has gotten way too personal."

She tossed him that sexy smile as she went to him. "Patrick, tonight I went to a seminar at the Healthy Living Clinic in Portland and attended a water aerobics class." She reached out and placed her hand on his arm. "I could never be with another man, not after what we shared."

"Dammit, Cyndi. Don't say that," he pleaded, fighting hard not to grab her.

In the dim light he could see her whiskey-brown eyes. "It's true. I never expected to see you again after that night. I left because I was afraid of what you would think… I was the one who seduced you."

Like she was doing to him now. "This isn't a good idea," he said. "You and me." It was too late; he lost the battle and drew her against him. He leaned closer and placed a kiss on her lips, then pulled back. He closed his eyes, momentarily savoring her. "Damn, you taste good. You smell good, too." He inhaled deeply. "I'm about at the end of my patience."

Cynthia put her arms around his neck, not wanting Patrick to pull away again. "I don't want your patience. I want you."

He gave her that look that took her breath away, then he lowered his head and his mouth captured hers. Sensation raced through her, and she heard the sound of her own moans as his hands journeyed down to her bottom, pulling her against his aroused body. He coaxed her mouth open, and she felt a shocked delight as he slipped his tongue inside to dance with hers.

His fingers were slow, yet eager to touch her. They moved under her T-shirt and cupped her breasts through her bra. She wanted more contact and worked at the snaps on his shirt until she could feel his warm skin.

It was his turn to groan as he broke off the kiss.

"You are sin, Cyn." His breath caressed her face, then he trailed kisses along her jaw and moved to her ear. "Damn, what is that perfume you have on? It makes me crazy."

Cynthia's smile widened. All she had on was her NoWait oil. "I guess I need to put it all over my body."

He groaned again. "You're killing me."

"Oh, no. We can't have that. I've got plans for you."

He raised his head and smiled at her. The old Patrick was back. "And what are those plans?"

"You still need to teach me to ride."

He cocked an eyebrow. "I believe you know how to ride."

Before she could react to his sexual innuendo, his mouth crushed hers once again. This time his need had intensified; his hunger was evident. He broke off the kiss, his breathing rough. "I want you, Cyndi."

"I want you, too."

Patrick took her hand and led her into the tack room. He knew he was acting crazy, but he wasn't about to stop. He flipped on a single light in the center of the small room, then led her to a cot on the back wall.

"It's not the Grand Hotel, but I can't wait to have you."

"I feel the same way," she breathed as he began taking off her blouse, then stripped off his shirt and tossed it on the floor. He stopped and kissed her once again as they worked at removing the rest of their clothing.

Hearing a noise, he suddenly froze and drew Cyndi against him. "Listen. Someone is in the barn." Leaving her at the bunk, he grabbed his shirt and went to investigate. Out in the center aisle he found Forest checking on the horses.

Patrick had forgotten that his foreman always did a walk-through before he retired for the night.

"Hey, Pat. What are you doing out here?" he asked.

"Just getting some fresh air before I turn in," Patrick said, lousy at lying. He wasn't about to broadcast that he was with Cyndi. Not that Forest would say anything.

Hell, he was the one who was crazy. He drew a deep breath and released it. Sex in the barn. What had he been thinking? That was the problem, he hadn't been using his brain at all. Not when Cyndi was around anyway. Thank God he'd come to his senses.

After he watched his foreman leave, he returned to the tack room to find Cyndi sitting on the cot. He was relieved that she'd put on her blouse.

"It was Forest," he told her.

"Is everything okay?"

He nodded. "Maybe we should get back to the house. We have an early day tomorrow."

Cyndi blinked in surprise, but he didn't give her a chance to argue as he led her out of the room. Things got a little more complicated when they got to the house. He stopped in the kitchen, trying not to look at her mussed hair and her swollen lips.

"You should go up to bed. You've got a busy day tomorrow." He glanced away from the hurt look on her face. "And I have some paperwork to finish up."

She hesitated and he felt his resolve weakening. He wanted nothing more than to follow her and crawl into bed with her. She finally nodded then went upstairs. This was for the best, he told himself. He wasn't cut out for relationships, for that happily ever after.

But for once in his life he truly wanted it.

For the first time since she'd arrived at Tanner Ranch, Cynthia wanted to stay in bed. She didn't want to face Patrick. His rejection had hurt her. How dare he play with her emotions? She wanted to think it didn't matter, but Patrick had come to mean a lot to her. More than she wanted him to.

Cynthia thought back to their night together. He'd been so free with his caresses, his loving. That first night she'd believed he could care about her. So how could he reject her so easily now? Was this payback because she'd left him in the hotel room?

Five more days, Cynthia thought as she got dressed in her jeans and boots. After pulling her hair into a ponytail, she applied sunscreen, then headed for the door. She stopped and grabbed her NoWait oil off the dresser and quickly put some on. Even though she wasn't irresistible to Patrick, she liked her new trim body.

Downstairs, Cynthia was surprised when she found Patrick in the kitchen. He was at the stove cooking breakfast, and when he glanced over his shoulder, her stomach did a somersault. Darn, there was that feeling again.

"Good morning."

She wasn't ready for this. "Good morning," she managed, wondering how she was going to get through the next few days. "What can I do to help?"

"Nothing. It's my turn to cook." He carried two plates to the table and sat down across from her.

Cynthia tried to concentrate on her food, but she couldn't seem to get the eggs down. Instead, she pushed them around on her plate as Patrick talked about the morning routine.

There was a long, silent pause, then he spoke again. "About what happened last night," he began.

"Nothing happened," she said.

He raised an eyebrow. "A lot happened. And I'm sorry. I promised that we'd stick to business."

Her heart ached. "Please, don't apologize. We both got carried away. It won't happen again." She got up and carried her plate to the sink, then walked out the door.

A tear ran down her cheek, and she brushed it away. She only had five more days then she'd be gone, hopefully busy with her movie project. She wouldn't have to worry about Patrick Tanner anymore. Suddenly more tears streamed down her face and she couldn't stop them. This time she didn't even try.

That evening Cynthia had left Patrick a note. As promised, she let him know that she wouldn't be there for dinner. Once again she went to the clinic, in an effort to concentrate on Dr. Richie's lecture on self-esteem.

When applause broke out, Cynthia realized she hadn't heard much of the talk. She stood and was beginning to file out of the room, when a woman moved through the crowd toward her.

She was young and slender, with long straight brown hair. She had pretty eyes, but they were partially hidden by oversize glasses. A little makeup would help her pale complexion.

Cynthia had seen her many times before and knew she worked for Dr. Richie.

"Ms. Reynolds, I'm Abby Edwards. I'm Dr. Strong's PR representative."

"Hello, Ms. Edwards," Cynthia said and shook her hand.

"It's an honor to meet you. I'm such a big fan."

Cynthia had always had trouble handling her celebrity status. "Thank you."

"If you have a moment I would like to talk with you."

"Sure."

They separated themselves from the departing crowd.

Abby adjusted her glasses, then turned serious. "Dr. Richie wanted me to speak with you. He's so happy that you've been attending his seminars and using his oil. He would approach you himself but he's afraid he'll draw attention to you and he knows how important privacy is—to all his clients."

Cynthia was pleased. "I appreciate that he's so considerate. It's nice that I can come here and just be me." Sometimes she wondered who that was. She thought of Patrick. She found herself wishing she could be the woman he needed. Whoa, hold it right there, she thought. Since when did she need to rely on a man?

"If I may be so bold, Ms. Reynolds, you look terrific. Not that you didn't before, but there seems to be a glow about you. I hope you feel that Dr. Richie and NoWait have contributed to that."

"I do. I've never felt in better shape. As you know I already sent Dr. Richie a letter stating that."

Abby nodded. "And he was happy to receive it. Since you feel so strongly about the program, there is something else we would like you to consider. How would you feel about letting Dr. Richie use your name to promote the program?"

Cynthia was taken aback by the request. She had never done endorsements before, and wasn't crazy about doing this, even for Dr. Richie. "I'll need some time to consider it. So I'll have to get back to you."

"Of course, that's understandable." Abby Edwards smiled, then reached out her hand and Cynthia shook it. "I'll give you a call in…two weeks?"

"Sure. Goodbye." Cynthia turned to leave and saw Kelly coming into the room. They'd made a date to meet for dinner.

"When you didn't come out to the car, I wondered if I missed you."

"No, I was talking to Dr. Richie's PR person. She wants my endorsement of NoWait."

Kelly raised an eyebrow. "I hope you didn't say you'd do it."

"Of course not." Together they walked through the doors into the hall, passing several couples holding hands, or with their arms around each other. Some pairs were boldly exchanging kisses. "I said I'd get back to her in a few weeks. I'll just hand it over to my lawyer." She smiled sweetly. Although her sister was a divorce lawyer, she handled a lot of Cyndi's affairs.

"Good, this NoWait oil hasn't been thoroughly tested. I'd hate to see you on a TV infomercial selling the stuff, then end up being sued."

"Always the practical one."

"Someone has to be." They pushed through the doors that led to the parking lot.

People turned as they walked by. She was recognized, but most fans just smiled at her, a few asked for autographs, and she willingly obliged.

"Where do you want to eat?" Kelly asked.

"I don't care. Just someplace quiet. I really don't feel like being bothered tonight."

Kelly sighed. "Well, that's what you get for being famous."

Cynthia thought about her life. She'd been doing that a lot lately. Maybe it was because she'd turned thirty-five and time seemed to be slipping away. She had no one special to share it with—no husband…no children.

"Kel, did you ever wish your life had gone in another direction? That you hadn't become a lawyer?"

Kelly paused at the driver's side of her Mercedes. "The only other thing I wanted to be years ago was a fireman." She shrugged. "I love being a lawyer, but I've been thinking about doing more pro bono work. Forest has been telling me about the shelter kids."

"Forest!"

"Yes, Forest." Kelly climbed in the car.

A surprised Cynthia got in the passenger side. "I didn't know you were seeing Forest."

"We haven't exactly been *seeing* each other." She put the key in the ignition and started the car. "Okay, we had dinner once, and he brought me lunch at the office." She smiled. "No man has ever done that for me."

Cynthia was envious and happy at the same time. "You deserve special treatment."

"Anyway, he suggests I donate time for the kids at the shelter."

"Some of those kids were at the ranch the other day. Patrick and Nora have been teaching them to ride." Cynthia thought about Davy, wondering how he was doing, whether someone was taking care of him, reading him a story and tucking him into bed at night. Or if he was afraid. She shivered. "I got to help, too. So you're serious about helping out?"

"Yeah," her sister announced. "It'll be a nice change from couples bickering over who gets the beach house or the cabin cruiser." She raised a hand. "Okay, so their money keeps me in a lifestyle I've come to love. But I'm realizing there's something I've missed in my life."

From an early age, Kelly had been the original material girl. "Oh, my, that's quite a revelation." Cynthia was thinking the same.

Her sister glanced in her direction, then pulled out onto the street. "What about you, sis? There was a time when you wanted to teach school. I know Mom had pushed you to keep making movies, and we all relied heavily on your financial support, especially me for college. I always wondered if you gave up your dream to give me mine."

"Oh, Kelly, no." She touched her sister's arm. "I was happy that I made enough money to help out the family. If I'd wanted to go to college, I could have."

Kelly looked doubtful. "Mom didn't exactly make the decision easy for you. She was good at encouraging guilt. You've made her life pretty comfortable. You've even helped our father. God, I hate to call that man that."

"I just helped that one time."

Cynthia remembered when their father had called her out of the blue. In the previous twelve years he'd never called or paid child support. And they had gone without a lot as kids. She'd ended up giving him money, but only after he promised to stay out of their lives.

"You bought him a house."

"And it's all the way across the country," Cynthia stressed. "He would have sold his story to the media and made our lives a living hell. It was simpler to help him out."

"When is it going to be time for you, sis? When do you take time for some happiness?"

She laughed. "You make me sound like a martyr. I do plenty for me. I've had a great career."

"But are you happy, Cyn? I don't think you have been for a long time. You're in a rough business. It's cruel and you deserve better. I think finding Patrick could be a good beginning."

"What are you talking about? Patrick Tanner is teaching me to ride. There's no beginning." Cynthia had to push aside any dreams of a man like Patrick in her life. He wanted nothing to do with an actress.

"Not according to Forest. He says Patrick has feelings for you. Of course, he's just as stubborn as you."

Cynthia would love it if that were true. "One minute Patrick can barely stand having me around, then the next he's kissing me. It's confusing. As things stand now, there's no future for us."

"Never say never. Forest let it slip that there was a woman in Patrick's past. She did quite a number on him and he doesn't trust easily. You could change that."

"No, I'm staying clear of the man." Cynthia had had her fill of his rejection. She didn't need him telling her again that he didn't want her.

Why did love have to hurt so badly? Her heart tightened in her chest. Oh, God, no. She sucked in a gasp. She couldn't be falling in love with the man. But it looked like it was too late. She was well on her way.

Seven

The following day, as usual, Cynthia had gotten up at six o'clock and was downstairs by six-thirty. For a change she decided to fix bacon-and-egg sandwiches for breakfast. She knew that she should be watching her diet, but with the amount of exercise she'd been doing and her NoWait oil, she could splurge a little.

She had also increased her muscle tone, especially in her legs and rear end. She rubbed her tender bottom. All this was due to the fact that she'd been riding a horse. No wonder cowboys had such great-looking backsides.

When Patrick came through the back door she tried not to be affected by his overwhelming presence, but it didn't work. Her pulse pounded in her veins as she gave his well-toned body the once-over. She'd worked with a lot of the leading men in Hollywood, but it was Patrick Tanner who made her lose control. Lord, he had her hormones doing a jig.

"Good morning," she managed.

"Good morning," he greeted her and took off his hat, causing his blond-streaked hair to fall across his forehead. Cynthia had trouble drawing air into her lungs when he ambled over to the coffeemaker. She quickly took the bread from the toaster and slapped together the makings of a sandwich. Just a few more days and she'd be gone. There would be an end to the temptation.

"I made us egg sandwiches."

Patrick leaned a hip against the counter and took a sip of his coffee. "Sounds good," he lied. It didn't matter what she cooked, he hadn't had any appetite lately. He eyed Cyndi's shapely little backside in her jeans and his body stirred. Not for food. He went to the table and sat down. That wasn't any better. She sat across from him, giving him a perfect view of those incredible brown eyes and that sexy mouth.

Food. He needed to concentrate on food. He reached for his sandwich and took a huge bite, but his gaze was drawn back to her. His eyes lingered on her slender hands and long fingers as she held the bread. Her nails were short. His gaze returned to her face, scrubbed clean of any makeup, her red hair pulled into a no-nonsense braid. There was no sign of the pampered Hollywood starlet he'd once thought she was. Cyndi had worked hard, both at riding and ranch chores, and without complaint.

Patrick identified the problem. He wanted her. Had done every day, every minute since that night at Morgan's. Nothing he'd done had made it stop, either. For the past few days he'd tried to keep his distance. It wouldn't have been so hard if he hadn't had the memories of their one night together. But he'd already known what it was like to touch her, caress her flawless skin, then sink deep inside her. He groaned.

She looked at him. "Something wrong?"

He shook his head. "Just eating too fast." He swallowed hard. "We've got a lot to do today. Are you up for a ride outside the corral?"

Her chocolate eyes rounded. "You mean it?"

Patrick found her excitement contagious. "Yeah. I think it's time I broadened your horizon. So let's go get saddled up." He stood, took his plate to the sink and she followed. When she started to rinse the dishes, he reached for her hand to stop her. The electrical shock nearly threw him backward.

She frowned. "What?"

Patrick released her. "Leave them. I'll do 'em later." She followed him to the door. He grabbed his hat, then handed one to her. "Come on, the sun's up."

Twenty minutes later, Forest held open the gate that led out to the open pasture and Cynthia walked Daisy toward the trail. The high grass waved in the summer breeze. Rows and rows of tall pine trees met the majestic mountain range, and the crowning glory was the clear blue sky. Cynthia sat in the saddle, holding Daisy's reins, but the scenery had her attention until Patrick rode up beside her.

"How do you feel?"

She couldn't hold back her smile. "Great. This is a whole different world than any I've ever known. I grew up in the city with noise, smog and freeway traffic." She drew another deep breath. "This is heaven."

"I feel the same. I don't know if I could ever live anywhere else."

"You were lucky you had parents who wanted their kids to have this kind of life."

She watched the light fade from his eyes. "Yeah, I was lucky. Maybe we should get to work on the lesson. I have a lot of other things to do today."

"I'm ready," she said, trying not to let his sudden mood change bother her.

"Okay. Let's pick up the pace." He kicked his horse's side, and Cynthia did the same. She was determined to keep up with him. Daisy cooperated and obeyed her every command. Cynthia felt the wind in her hair as she began to canter, trying to remember how to sit, to be one with the horse. For a while she bounced up and down, then finally caught the horse's rhythm.

Patrick rode up beside her and critiqued her posture, then urged her to go faster. She lowered her head and nudged Daisy's sides and they shot off. After about a hundred yards, Patrick called to her to stop. She pulled back on the reins and slowed at the edge of the trees.

She turned around and saw Patrick come up. "Well, how did I do?"

"Not bad."

"Not bad!" She worked to slow her breathing. "A week ago I wouldn't have come near a horse, let alone ride one."

"I know and you're doing great, but you have

to work on your posture some more. You're a little stiff. A few more days of practice and you should look a lot better."

He rode ahead of her and Daisy followed. "Where are we going?" she asked. The trail led them under the tall trees that filtered out most of the sunlight, and the temperature dropped.

"You ask a lot of questions," he called over his shoulder.

"And my mother taught me never to go off into the woods with men." After a while the sun again brightened their path as the trees changed. Now they were smaller and planted in neat rows that seemed to go on forever.

"You're not in the woods anymore. You're in the middle of the Tanner Christmas Tree Farm."

"I thought you raised horses."

"Ranch land has to be multipurpose to survive these days. I raise cattle and horses, grow trees and have been known to plant a few crops."

"I'm impressed," she said. "You have quite an operation."

Patrick shifted in the saddle. He didn't like to talk about his business, but Cyndi's interest drew the words from him. "We do what we have to do," he told her. "I had sisters to care for, so there wasn't much of a choice. I didn't want to lose our home." He'd been too close to that possibility twice and he never wanted to be there again.

He shook away the thought. "There's a line shack up on the ridge. We'll stop there and rest the horses."

He should just turn around and take her back to the barn, but he wasn't ready to end this time with her.

They pulled up in front of a crude structure. About twenty yards away was a small stream, so he hobbled the horses and let them drink and graze.

"When I hire a crew to cut the trees, we use this place as the base." He walked her up to the porch, wondering what she thought about the simple shack.

"Oh my, it's like I've stepped back in time about a hundred years. How old is this place?"

"Not sure. It's been around since my dad was a kid."

The cabin had been his escape from Michael Tanner when he went on a drunken rage. More than once, it had been a safe haven where he'd brought his sisters to hide. He only wished he could have found a way to save his mother. That pang of guilt would always be with him.

Patrick pushed open the door and allowed Cyndi to go in ahead of him. The inside was anything but fancy. Just a scarred table, a few mismatched chairs and built-in bunk beds up against the far wall, with rolled-up bedding on the metal springs. The kitchen area had a couple of cabinets, and a rust-pitted sink with a pump that drew its water from a well. Heat was supplied by a potbellied stove, and Patrick had bought a generator a few years back so they would have electricity.

"It's not the Ritz, or your mansion in Hollywood."

Cynthia swung around. "You really must think I'm such a snob." Her eyes flashed. "I'll have you know that you'd be appalled at some of the places Kelly and I had to live in when we were kids. Our father walked out on us years ago, and our mother couldn't seem to hold a job—or her second husband or her third." She shrugged. "Of course Kelly and I were happy when she stopped bringing strange men into our lives—men who always seemed to take an unhealthy interest in her young daughters."

Patrick cursed and started toward her, but she backed away.

"So don't go assuming you know me," she spat out as she turned and walked out the door.

Patrick drew a frustrated breath and released it. She was right. He didn't really know Cynthia Reynolds. Suddenly he found he did want to know everything about her.

He walked out to the porch. She faced away from him looking out toward the creek. "You're right, Cyndi. I shouldn't have judged you."

She shook her head. "No, I apologize. I have no idea what got into me. I've made a considerable amount of money in the movie business. And I do have a nice home in L.A. Not a mansion, just a nice house. I'm not a showy person. And I will always remember where I came from."

He'd never forget his past, either. He had his father's legacy to remind him. "I don't think our childhood ever leaves us."

"No, I guess that makes us who we are."

She looked so vulnerable and that made him vulnerable. She made him feel so many things, a connection for one. But their lives were so different. She'd be going back to Hollywood, and she'd forget he ever existed. No, they didn't have a future, but that didn't stop the wanting.

Cynthia felt like throttling Patrick, but she also wanted him. How could she desire him so much when he was such a crazy-maker, one minute kissing her, the next minute pushing her away.

He closed the distance between them and surprised her when he reached for her. Her heart drummed in her chest as he drew her against him. She never knew whether this man was going to run hot or cold, but when he touched her, she didn't care. His head lowered to hers and he captured her mouth. She thought she was going to melt there on the spot, but he held her up, holding her against him.

He broke off the kiss. "This is dangerous," he whispered, just before his mouth returned to hers. Teasing her lips apart, he pushed his tongue inside to taste her. She moaned as his arms wrapped tighter, holding her close, causing her to feel the imprint of his arousal. Then suddenly he released her.

His breathing was ragged and his eyes didn't hide his desire. "You are one sexy woman, Cyndi. We better get back or I'm going to break my promise to you."

Before Cynthia could say anything, he walked off the porch and headed for the horses. Okay, maybe he was right. He wanted her, but he'd let her know there wasn't any future for them. That was one of the things she admired about this man—his integrity.

Only not right now.

* * *

That evening, Carrie Martin found herself back at the Healthy Living Clinic attending another meeting. This time the evening seminar was packed. Standing room only. She recognized several faces in the crowd, famous people like Cynthia Reynolds. Carrie almost didn't realize it was the actress without her makeup and styled hair. Like most of the people here, she was dressed casually, having come from working out in the fitness center.

Carrie was still amazed that her ex-husband had caused such a stir in Portland. His new product was the buzz throughout the clinic, and she'd even heard rumors about it going national. People had nothing but praise for the doctor. She tensed. She wondered how they'd all feel if they knew the truth about their precious Dr. Richie. He was a womanizer and an absentee father.

Carrie's thoughts turned to her late husband, Ralph. For fifteen years he'd loved her dearly, and she'd loved him, but they'd both known that someone had stood between them. Richard.

Even when Ralph had been dying, his only worry had been for her and Jason. She hadn't deserved her husband, because she'd still carried feelings for the man who'd deserted her and their child.

And Dr. Richie needed to pay the price for what he'd done.

All in due time, she told herself. She wasn't ready yet to announce her presence back in his life.

Around midnight, Patrick wasn't in a good mood. He'd spent the evening with Nora, who'd been far too curious about what was going on. She had asked too many questions, especially about Cyndi. Where had she gone tonight? When was she coming home? He wanted to know the same things, but Cyndi hadn't told him a thing. There had only been a note that said she wouldn't be home for dinner. Why should she tell him anything? He'd pushed her away so many times. He didn't have a claim on her.

Not that he didn't want to lay claim, but in the long run, this was best for both of them. He reminded himself of that as he stood under the cool shower spray, hoping to ease the tension in his body. He'd never gotten so aroused by a woman that he couldn't concentrate on one damn thing. He hated that Cyndi had that power. She'd managed to be on his mind too much. During the day, he'd find himself thinking about her; at night he dreamed about her lying next to him...about making love to her.

Stop it! He shut off the water and stepped out of the stall. After drying off, he wrapped the towel around his waist, then raked his fingers through his wet hair as he walked into his bedroom. He needed sleep. He'd worked hard today so there shouldn't be any reason he couldn't fall off once his head hit the pillow.

Yeah, right. Patrick had just jerked the blanket back when a sudden noise alerted him that someone was in the house. Cyndi. So she'd come home. There was a crash and then her cry, sending him running into the hall. He flipped on the light and looked over the banister to find Cyndi sprawled at the bottom of the stairs along with a toppled end table.

Patrick hurried down to see if she was injured. When she tried to move, he stopped her. "Lie still. You could be hurt."

"I'm okay. I'm sorry about the table and the photos."

"The hell with the furniture. What about you?"

"I only fell down two steps and landed on my butt." She grimaced. "Sorry I woke you. I was trying to be quiet."

He helped her sit up. "And you could have hurt yourself in the process. Of all the crazy things…" He eased her to her feet. "The hall light wouldn't wake me. Hell, I wasn't even in bed yet."

"You should be. You have to get up at five."

"It's a little late to worry about that now."

She jerked away from his hold. "And what's that supposed to mean?"

"Hell, woman, I haven't had a decent night's sleep since I met you."

She stared at him, anger flashing in her eyes. "And that's my problem? You're blaming me for your lack of sleep? That's just great." She grabbed her purse and marched up the stairs. Her shapely bottom swayed back and forth, heightening his desire. "Good night, Patrick. Sweet dreams," she taunted as she disappeared into her room, slamming the door behind her.

Patrick closed his eyes. She had him in so many knots that he wasn't going to survive another day—hell, another minute. He climbed the stairs two at a time and stormed to her room.

Hearing the loud pounding on her door, Cynthia jumped. Patrick. Well, she was in the mood for a fight. She'd barely got the door open when Patrick grabbed her and pulled her to him.

His eyes bored into hers. "If you have any protests, you'd better tell me now, because I'm going to make love to you and I'm not stopping until I get my fill."

Cynthia's heart was pounding erratically as she reached up and ran her fingers through his hair. "No. You're not stopping until I get *my* fill."

She tugged his mouth down to hers, capturing his hunger, thrilled that it was all for her. She pressed her body against his near-naked form and got a groan from him. He kissed so well. His tongue plunged deep into her mouth and dueled with hers. This time *she* moaned, hoping to get more. She did. His hand moved down to clamp on her bottom, his fingers digging into her. Her skin was set on fire as his hands moved over her body, all the time his lips working their own magic.

He tore his mouth from hers but continued to spread kisses across her face and into her ear, making her shiver and sway in his arms.

"Whoa, unless you want to finish this up on the floor," he said.

"So are you going to finish this time?" she managed.

"That's the plan. Any objections?"

"Not a one," she answered.

He began walking her backward until she felt her legs hit the edge of the bed. Then they both tumbled and landed with a bounce. "New mattress." He cocked an eyebrow. "I think we're going to give it a workout tonight."

"Think so?" she teased, wanting to believe everything he was telling her.

He nodded, his hair falling across his forehead.

Then he dipped his head and began taking teasing nibbles from her lips till finally deepening the kiss. When he raised his head, his breathing was rough. "I think one of us has too many clothes on."

Cynthia ran the back of her hand against his jaw and inhaled his familiar scent of soap and man. "Should I change into a towel?"

He smiled and her stomach tightened. "How about I just give you mine? But first, I'm going to strip every piece of clothing off you," he promised, emphasizing each word with a breathy pause as his skilled hand slid down her body.

He climbed off the bed and bent down to remove her sandals, then unfastened her slacks, and in his enthusiasm, nearly pulled her off the mattress. Next came her T-shirt, and she sat there in her sheer bra and panties. Her nipples hardened in delight as his gaze moved over her, examining her closely.

When she was finally naked, he said, "You're as beautiful as I remembered."

So was he. His body was rock-hard, and a light sheen of perspiration covered his bare chest. Unable to wait any longer, Cynthia reached out and hooked her finger in his towel, then yanked it off. Seeing his powerful arousal, she felt her body tingle. "And I never forgot how beautiful you are." She leaned back on the bed and held out her arms to him. "I don't think we need a towel, do you?"

Patrick stretched over her and placed a kiss on her lips, then began kissing his way down her throat and over the slope of her breast. "No way. I like you just like this." He cupped her breast, then clamped his mouth over one hard nipple and sucked it. A shock wave went through all the way to her stomach, causing her to arch her hips as goose bumps rose along her skin.

"I love the way you respond to me."

Cynthia was almost afraid to move, but her body reacted automatically and she bucked against him as his tongue continued to work her into a frenzy. And she wanted even more.

He leaned over her, spreading her hands on either side of her head, pinning them to the mattress. Without breaking their linked gazes, he leaned down and used his tongue on her skin. Once again, his mouth moved down her body. She arched her back when his tongue plunged into her navel.

"You like that?" He repeated the action.

She gasped, feeling her body tense in anticipation, moisture pooling between her legs. "More. I need…"

Suddenly his body pressed into hers as his

mouth met hers in an all-consuming kiss. When he raised his head, he was breathing hard.

"Tell me what you need."

"You."

His tongue dipped into her mouth while his hands parted her thighs and his fingers slipped inside her.

She gasped, but couldn't speak. She grabbed the mattress and opened more for him.

"You like that, Cyn?"

Nodding, she closed her eyes and tried to grasp reality. She'd never felt so helpless and didn't care. Then he bent down and replaced his fingers with his mouth, torturing her even further with flicks of his tongue. It only took a few strokes to bring her to the edge and she cried out.

Patrick was about to climb out of his skin, he wanted her so badly. He leaned over her, kissed her lips, then when she opened her eyes and smiled at him, he nearly lost it.

"Make love to me, Patrick."

"My pleasure. I'll be right back." He disappeared, but within seconds he returned to her side. He held up a foil packet. A condom. He quickly prepared himself, all the while telling himself to go slow. He wanted this woman so desperately that his control was nil. Silently he shifted between her thighs and in a swift motion slipped inside her. With a gasp, she wrapped her legs around him as he began to move in strong, controlled strokes, savoring her tight body.

Cyndi would have none of it. She grabbed his hips and pulled him in deeper, increasing the pace until he got caught up in the hunger. He couldn't get enough of her. Every stroke had him wanting more...much, much more. Her heat was scalding him and he couldn't endure it any longer. He picked up the pace, forcing them both closer and closer to the moment when it all became too much. Soon he felt himself building toward his climax, and when Cyndi tightened around him, he couldn't stop the intensity of his feelings.

He finally lost the battle and pushed inside her one more time, letting the pleasure carry him over the edge. He groaned and captured her cries with his mouth as he wrapped her in his arms.

That was when he knew he never wanted to let her go...but he knew that soon he had to.

He rolled to one side and held her until she drifted off to sleep. He kissed her hair and wondered what he could do to keep her by his side. It was impossible. The day was fast approaching when she'd leave and never look back.

With his heart aching, Patrick resigned himself to savoring the moment.

Eight

Patrick hadn't moved away from Cyndi and he never wanted to. Ever. His body was spent, but his mind was working overtime. She would be gone in a matter of days. But right now this woman was lying naked in his arms and he didn't want to think beyond this moment.

Her hand moved over his chest as she stirred against him. "Tell me you're not having regrets," she murmured. It surprised him to hear an unsure tone in her soft voice.

He leaned over her. "I have a lot of regrets, but

making love to you isn't one of them." He placed a kiss on her mouth. "I thought our first time together was wild, but damn, there were a couple times now I thought my heart had stopped." He laughed and lay back down. "Aren't we a strange pair? The actress and the rancher."

This time Cyndi raised her head, her gaze on his. "Patrick…"

When he turned to her, she began, "It's important that you know I don't normally hop into bed with men I've only known for hours or a few days." She drew her eyebrows together as her fingers began to move over his skin. "That's the reason I'm so baffled that I can't seem to keep my hands off you."

He grinned to try and lighten the mood. "I guess Oregon cowboys just have a way with women." Her touch was torturing him.

"You have a way with me, Patrick Tanner."

"That works both ways, Cyn." He turned her in his arms and ended up on top of her. He hadn't wanted to care so much for her, but he couldn't seem to stop it. Already his body was betraying him by wanting her again. He felt exposed and defenseless. Yet one look into her large brown eyes told him she was just as vulnerable.

Patrick lowered his head and captured her

mouth, then began to nibble on her lower lip. He loved to taste her…all over. She circled her arms around his neck then drew him closer. He deepened the kiss as he rubbed himself up and down against her body. There was that catch in her breath as the familiar urgency took over. He rolled on his back, taking her with him, and positioned her on top of him…filling her. He shut everything else out of his mind. Nothing else mattered but her.

Right before dawn, Cynthia opened her eyes and immediately knew she wasn't alone. She smiled, feeling Patrick's naked body pressed against her back, his arm draped over her, his hand covering her breast.

Even if she wanted to, she couldn't leave. But she had no intention of going anywhere. She was going to spend as much time as possible with the man she'd fallen hopelessly in love with. She'd been fighting the attraction for days now, but after last night there was no doubt about her feelings.

Now, if Patrick would only give her a clue as to how he felt. Her chest tightened and she closed her eyes, recalling the pleasure he had given her. He had to care about her.

His hand on her breast moved in a slow caress as his lower body shifted against hers, then he placed a kiss on her neck. She moaned as her need began to grow. She could get used to this, she thought as she turned in his arms.

The room was still dim, but she could clearly see his smile as he looked down at her.

"Good, you aren't a dream."

She smiled back. "You sure?" she teased as her arms circled his neck.

"My dreams usually end by morning," he said, reminding her of how she'd left him in the hotel after their first night together.

She shook her head. "This is another dream. I even stay through the whole day."

He kissed the end of her nose. "I like this dream. What's next?"

"That's the good part. You get to chose how your dream plays out. You can make me disappear or…have me stay."

He groaned. "What do you want?"

She lowered her eyes. "It's your dream. You choose."

"Give me a minute to think about it." Patrick liked the game-playing, he also liked waking up with Cynthia in his arms. It wouldn't take much to get used to her being around. He'd never realized how lonely he'd been until she ended up living in his house, sleeping down the hall from him.

In reality, he knew she was leaving in a matter of days, and he wasn't crazy enough to think she'd stay after her lessons were finished. Besides, he couldn't get any more involved than he already was. This couldn't lead to anything permanent. They only had now.

"How about we spend the day in bed?"

She smiled at him in that sexy, playful way she had. "I'd like that, too, but wouldn't your animals get hungry?"

He stole another kiss. "Not as hungry as I am for you." He kissed her again, this time a little longer, a little deeper. "And I'm definitely hungry." He went back for another taste as his body shifted over her. He was breathing hard when he broke off the kiss. "What about you?"

"Me, too," she whispered as she rose up and kissed him, her mouth hot, promising wild things.

Patrick thought he was going to explode from waiting, but he needed more from her. "You, too, what?" he asked.

Those sexy bedroom eyes of hers locked on his. "I'm hungry for you, Patrick Tanner. And if you don't make love to me right now, I'm going to go crazy."

"Let me see if I can do something about that."

He groaned as he slipped into her and began to move slowly.

He drove aside all his fears and doubts. They only had a short time together. The last thing he could think about was a future with Cyndi. It just wasn't possible.

Over an hour later, Patrick made his way to the kitchen, wanting to be upstairs with Cyndi. After they'd made love in bed, they ended up in the shower. When lathering up, they discovered their appetite for each other hadn't diminished at all. It took the water turning cold and the waiting chores to make them get out.

Whistling, Patrick pushed the button to start the coffeemaker, then he pulled eggs and bacon from the refrigerator. He lit the fire under the skillet and started on breakfast. He was still amazed how easily Cyndi had made him forget everything. If there had been one thing he'd always done, it was take his responsibilities seriously. He glanced at his watch. He was an hour late to feed the stock. Yet he was sure that Forest could handle things this one time.

Patrick had never had a real childhood. As the oldest child, and the only boy, he'd had to do endless chores, mostly because his dad had gotten drunk and was passed out in bed. It had gotten progressively worse over the years, and by fifteen, Patrick was running the ranch, trying hard to keep the place from going under. There hadn't been time for him to date or go out for sports during high school. He'd been needed at home.

Patrick felt his body tense as he cracked the eggs in the skillet. He'd never resented having to work, but he sure as hell had resented his old man for inflicting his brutality on his family. The life he'd forced on his wife, daughters and son. People said he was sick, but Patrick had only known Mick Tanner as cruel.

Cynthia stood in the doorway and studied Patrick as he worked in the kitchen. He wore jeans and a blue plaid shirt and his hair was wet from their shower together. The one that had nearly flooded the bathroom. Just the memory of the wonderful things this man had done to her under the spray of water had her stomach doing a flip-flop.

How was she going to be able to leave him? She pushed the sad thought out of her head. There were only a few days remaining with Patrick, and she was going to enjoy them. Even if they would be all she had.

She walked up behind him and snaked her arms

around his waist. "There's nothing sexier than a domesticated man, especially when he's cooking for me."

He turned around and grinned. "It's only fair since you washed my…back in the shower." He leaned down and kissed her. A short one that only left her wanting more. And she did want more from the man. So much more.

Patrick set her aside. "Now go away, woman. You're distracting the cook."

"So the truth comes out. Food comes first." She headed to the cupboard and took out plates and mugs.

"A man has to replenish his strength."

He glanced over his shoulder and sent her the look. The look that made her want to stop what she was doing and strip out of her clothes and make love to him right here.

When she came to her senses, she managed to say, "Well, then, let's eat." Her hands shook as she poured coffee. Handing him a cup, she carried hers to the table. She needed some distance from him before she did something foolish.

A few minutes later Patrick brought their breakfast to the table. He sat down across from her and concentrated on eating, making the silence stretch between them. Cynthia tried to push aside the uncertainty of this relationship, but it kept intruding. There was so much Patrick kept to himself. If she'd been wise, she would never have invited Patrick into her room last night. But it wouldn't have mattered if she'd locked him out. He'd already gotten into her heart.

Suddenly Patrick reached across the table and took her hand. "Now it's my turn to ask. Having regrets?"

She blinked. He was just as insecure as she was. She shook her head. "No."

He released an exaggerated breath. "Good. If you were, it sure would have messed up my plans for this morning."

"And what are those?"

Patrick shook his head. He took another bite of egg, then after he swallowed, he said, "If I told you, it wouldn't be my surprise." He ate some of his bacon. "You feel up to going for a ride this morning?"

She nodded. "Sure."

"Good, pack some sandwiches for our lunch while I go do chores. I'll be ready to leave in about an hour. How about you?"

"I think I could handle that."

He winked. "Good, I want to spend the day with you."

There it was again, the tightening in her chest. She was in big trouble.

That morning at the Healthy Living Clinic, Dr. Richard Strong was waiting in the wings while the audience filed in. He still had trouble believing his popularity. Not that he hadn't earned it. He'd worked hard to get to the top and he was enjoying every bit of it. The fame, the fortune…and the women.

People trusted him. He could see it in the faces of nearly every person who filled the auditorium. The women who stared lovingly at him. That was because they respected and trusted him. The men, too, were impressed with him. They even emulated him with similar hairstyles and gray suits.

Richard was flattered. In fact, he liked the gratitude he'd gotten from several lovely ladies. If he so desired, the famous Dr. Richie could have a different woman every night of the week. But after a while he'd found it had gotten old. He didn't remember names, but there hadn't been anyone special. It had been a long time since he'd truly cared about someone. Along with the fame came the loneliness. No one special to share all this with.

He thought back to a time when life had been

simpler…when he could go out, have a beer and play a game of pool. Just for fun. And back then there had been a woman who'd stood by him. Who'd loved him. At the time Richard hadn't thought she was enough.

In the meantime he'd have to settle for fame. He straightened his tie and strode to the podium.

As promised, Patrick returned to the house on time. Together, they went to the barn where Daisy and Ace were already saddled. After he'd put the food in saddlebags, they mounted and started off on the trail.

Once in the pasture, Cynthia checked the way she held the reins, wanting to do everything just right today. She knew Patrick was critiquing her as he rode beside her.

He turned in a different direction from their last ride and asked, "You ready to pick up the pace, or are you too tired?"

He was goading her. "I think I can handle anything you dish out, Mr. Tanner," she said.

He tossed her that sexy grin again. "I have no doubt." He kicked Ace's side and shot off.

Cynthia rode hard to keep up. "Come on, Daisy girl, we can't let the guys outdo us." The horse seemed to hear her and picked up speed.

She loved the feel of the wind in her hair and against her face. She'd never felt so free, so alive.

"Whoa, fella." Patrick slowed Ace, then turned in the saddle. Cyndi wasn't far behind. He found he enjoyed watching her. She had been a quick study. A natural. He only had to help her get over her fear.

"What's the matter, we wear you down?" Cyndi asked as she stopped beside him.

He leaned toward her and kissed her. "No, I just don't want you to spend all your energy on riding."

She blushed. "Don't worry about my energy. Now, where is this place?"

"Not far." He flipped his reins and changed direction. "Just follow me." They walked the horses through a thicket of trees. The shade cooled off the sunny summer day. Patrick was grateful there wasn't any rain forecast to spoil their picnic.

Finally they reached the edge of the rise, and he brought Ace to a stop. Cyndi came up beside him and looked down at the perfect rows of vines below.

She couldn't hide her surprise. "I didn't know you were in the wine business."

"I'm so new at it that I'm not sure I am. Forest and I just planted the rootstocks last spring. So far the Tanner Vineyard is an expensive venture. We eventually want to clear and plant more acreage, but we need to put in the trellis systems."

Daisy shifted, and Cyndi easily brought her back.

"What kind of wine grapes are you growing?"

"Pinot noir and chardonnay."

"This is the reason you agreed to teach me to ride."

Patrick nodded. "Starting a vineyard is expensive. The ranch does well, but I didn't want to borrow money from the operation just in case this venture didn't work out."

She smiled. "I'm glad I could help."

No matter how badly he needed the money, Patrick still felt bad about the amount she'd offered to pay him. "About the money. I can't take that much from you."

"So, I'm not the spoiled, pain-in-the-butt actress you first thought I was?"

He enjoyed the playful bantering. "You're a pain in the butt, but it's a cute butt."

"I'm glad you think so, but I'm still going to pay you what we agreed on. I don't renege on anything. Since you helped me with my dream, I'm happy to help you with yours."

"I'm not taking your money." He wasn't angry,

just stern. He tugged Ace's reins and turned around, then took off.

Cyndi was right on his heels, and by the time he reached the creek, she was nearly beside him. He slowed, then climbed down. She did the same and walked her horse to the water. "I'm going to pay you. We had a deal."

"That's before we made it personal."

"It was personal from that first night."

"I don't care. Dammit, I'm not taking your money."

She was silent for a long time, then said, "Would you take the studio's money?"

"What do you mean?"

"If I get this part in the movie, I'll make sure that it's put in my contract that you get paid for my riding lessons."

He frowned. "You can do that?"

She nodded. "Yes, I can. In fact, if you like, I can use your name as a reference and send you all kinds of business."

"Oh, no." He raised a hand. "I don't think I'm ready for that."

She looked him in the eye. "You mean you wouldn't want a bevy of Hollywood beauties hanging on your every word?"

No. He only wanted one beauty. He was itching to have her in his arms again. He couldn't touch her yet, or it would be all over. "I think one is plenty for me to handle."

"Oh, yeah? You think you can handle me?" She walked up to him with that dangerous, totally feminine rhythm that made his heart race.

He was in big trouble. "No, but I'm willing to give it one helluva try."

Cyndi stood close enough that he could smell her. Hot, sexy and all female. She made him hurt. She slid her hands around his waist, then stood up on her toes and pressed a kiss on his mouth. "I'm ready whenever you are."

It only took Patrick seconds to secure the horses, take the rolled blanket from his saddle and spread it on the grassy slope. Then he turned to her and held out a hand.

She didn't hesitate, and let him lead her to the blanket. He peeled her T-shirt over her head, then she removed his. He wanted her so desperately it frightened him. He could lie and say that it was because he hadn't been with anyone in a long time, but it was all Cyndi. He finished stripping off her clothes and laid her back, eager to get another taste of her.

Cynthia welcomed the kiss, taking everything he gave her. She couldn't explain what was happening and hated to analyze things. That was

Kelly's job. Even knowing Patrick could break her heart, she trusted him as she had trusted no other man. As much as he kept to himself, he didn't seem to have any trouble giving to her. His kisses grew more intimate; they traced from the soles of her feet up her legs to the heart of her. Patrick was taking her to that special place where no one else had ever taken her. She felt a rush of sensation when he moved over her and entered her body. Her spine arched, her pulse rushed as the feeling escalated within her. What she'd thought was only lust was so much more.

It was magic.

It had been an incredible day.

By afternoon, Patrick and Cyndi rode back to the corral. They'd probably stayed longer at the creek than they should have, but he hadn't played hooky in a long time. Years.

He couldn't help but grin as he thought back to how they'd spent their time. He should take a day off more often. Patrick glanced at Cyndi as she rode Daisy. Her hair was mussed and her cute nose was red from the sun. His gaze moved to her blouse as her breasts moved up and down with the rhythm of the horse. She smiled at him, and a rush of heat shot to his groin.

"You'd better stop looking at me that way, or we won't make it home for hours," he warned.

She laughed. "You are insatiable."

He shrugged. "I didn't hear you complaining."

"And you never will. Why don't we continue this back at the house?" she suggested. "The first one to the gate gets to shower first." She kicked her heels into Daisy and shot off.

Patrick was caught off guard by Cyndi's antics, but quickly made up the distance. Once close enough, he reached over and grabbed her around the waist, then pulled her off the galloping Daisy. Cyndi gasped as she ended up in his lap. He pulled up on the reins to slow his horse, then he lifted her tight against him, aware that she hadn't fought him as she'd been snatched from the saddle.

"Yeah, you move pretty smooth," he told her.

"Years of gymnastics. I've had to do a lot of stunts over the years." She settled against him. Her shapely bottom rested on his lap. Her arms went around his neck. "Now that you have me, what do you plan to do with me?"

He started to lean down to whisper in her ear when he saw the Mercedes sedan come down the road, then pull up at the house. Kelly Reynolds climbed out of the car.

He didn't even try to keep the disappointment from his voice. "I think we've got company."

Cynthia held on to Patrick as he lowered her from the horse. She retrieved Daisy, who had stopped just outside the corral fence.

"Come on, girl. You've had a busy day." She led the horse through the gate.

Patrick came up behind her and took her mount. "Go talk with your sister."

"I didn't know she was coming out." Cynthia frowned. Kelly wouldn't drive all the way out here unless it was important. "Maybe she's here to see Forest."

They both glanced toward the house and saw Forest greeting Kelly. "One can always hope," Patrick said.

"I'll see what she wants, then I'll take care of Daisy."

Patrick kissed her hard and quick. "I'd rather you come back and tend to me."

"Later," she promised, and took off to see Kelly.

Cynthia had been enjoying her stay in Portland. Normally she wasn't able to spend so much time with her sister. They both had busy careers.

She heard laughter as she approached the couple. "Sounds like you two are having fun."

Forest was the first to turn around. "I guess it's contagious. Have a nice ride?"

She blushed. "Yes, you have some beautiful country around here."

"And I bet Pat showed you the best places." His grin widened. "Well, I'll let you two visit." He looked at Kelly. "See you tomorrow night?"

Kelly nodded. "Seven o'clock."

The women watched as Forest walked away. He didn't look too bad either, Cynthia thought. His jeans encased muscular thighs and a tight rear, though not as nice as Patrick's. She figured Kelly might disagree.

"I take it the two of you are dating," she said finally.

"It's actually our first official date."

"So this thing between you and Forest, is it going somewhere?"

Kelly shrugged. "Could be. Did you know that Forest has an MBA and was a VP of a large software company? He gave it all up about eight years ago because it was consuming his life."

"No, I didn't know that. Life is full of surprises. Did anything else bring you out here?"

"Yeah, I'm heading over to the shelter for a consultation. Thought you'd like to go with me."

Cynthia looked toward the barn where Patrick

was brushing down one of the horses in the corral.

"Come on, your cowboy can get along without you for a few hours. I swear I'll have you back in time for supper."

Cynthia decided that since Patrick had spent the day with her, he probably needed to get things done. Besides, she didn't want him to think that she was too clingy—even if that was what she wanted to be. She wanted him to feel possessive about her, too.

"Sure, I'd love to go. I need a shower, and to tell Patrick." She started to walk toward the corral when her sister stopped her.

"I'm short on time. You go shower and I'll tell Patrick about our plans."

Reluctantly, Cynthia agreed, then walked off toward the house, already missing her cowboy.

"Cyndi, you came to see me," Davy Cooke cheered as he ran toward her in the shelter's lobby.

"Yes, I did." She knelt down to be at eye level with the seven-year-old. Her gaze raked over the boy, eager to gauge his well-being. "How have you been?"

"Okay. I haven't been in trouble one time, so I get to go ride with Patrick next time," he said proudly. "How's Daisy?"

"She's fine. I've been taking real good care of her."

Cynthia stood and looked around the government building, at the basic cream and green walls, the metal desks and worn furniture, the bare floors. At least Davy was healthy and well fed. But were those the most important things? What about a family? People to love him? Several other kids hung nearby, just close enough to share Davy's visitor. There were also counselors who were impressed to see the movie actress in their shelter. There were times when Cynthia liked her famous status, especially when she'd been allowed into a protected children's shelter.

The director of the shelter approached her. She was a woman of about forty with short brown hair and warm hazel eyes. "I'm Betty Moore. It's a pleasure to meet you, Miss Reynolds. I've been a fan of yours for so long."

They shook hands. "Please, call me Cyndi."

"I get to call her that, too," Davy said. "'Cause we're friends."

"We sure are," Cynthia agreed.

"Where's Patrick?" Davy asked.

"He's at the ranch, taking care of the horses. He has a lot of work to do. But you'll see him in a few days."

"I know, but I miss him. He's my friend." The boy's head lowered as he stared down at the floor. "He talks to me a lot." Then those big eyes met hers. "Guy stuff."

"That's good, because Patrick only has sisters and they don't talk guy stuff."

He nodded in agreement, then watched her a minute. "You like Patrick, too."

"Yes, I do. He's helping me learn to ride." Cynthia looked at Betty. "I'm going out for a movie role where I have to ride a horse. I'd appreciate it if you kept that to yourself."

"Oh, darn. I was hoping to make a million, selling that to the tabloids."

Cyndi grinned. "I doubt that info is worth that much."

One of the other boys yelled for Davy. He waved, then looked back at Cynthia. "I've gotta go. Will you come back and see me again?"

Betty sent her a warning look. Cyndi knew not to make any promises she might not be able to keep. "I'll try. Can I write you a letter?"

"Yeah, I guess that's cool." Davy put out his hand for her to shake.

Cynthia realized she wanted more. She leaned down. "Do you think we're good enough friends that I can have a hug?"

"Sure." He went into her open arms, but she felt him stiffen as if he were holding back his feelings. It broke her heart.

"I care about you, Davy," she whispered. "If you ever need anything, you just talk to Kelly." She pointed to her sister, who was talking with one of the counselors. "She'll be coming here every week. Or tell Nora. She can call me."

Davy nodded, then sadness clouded his eyes. "You're never going to come back and see me, are you?"

Cynthia didn't know how to answer him. She'd spent years avoiding any involvement. It had always been safer. A way to protect herself. But this little boy had gotten to her, and she couldn't abandon him. "I'm going to try."

That didn't seem to encourage him, but he nodded. Then he shot off to be with friends.

Cynthia brushed the tears from her eyes as she stood.

Betty put her hand on her arm. "These kids' stories will break your heart, but Davy especially got to us. He acts tough, but he's had a miserable life for someone so young."

"How do you do this all the time?" Cynthia asked.

"There are good days and bad days, but I love

these kids. And I hope that in some small way I help them." Betty looked at her and smiled. "You would make a good counselor. Ever think seriously about giving up fame and fortune to help out people like us?"

Cynthia realized she just might have more than one dream....

Nine

Cynthia came rushing through the back door around six that evening. She dropped the restaurant take-out on the counter and looked around, finding the kitchen empty. She was relieved that Patrick wasn't home yet. That would give her time to get dinner ready.

She'd talked Kelly into stopping off at an Italian restaurant in town to pick up dinner to go. Tonight, she wanted to make a quiet, romantic meal for just the two of them. She'd picked up a bottle of wine at a local winery and hoped that Patrick would like her effort. Kelly also had her own plans for Forest. She was bringing him supper at his place.

Cynthia quickly set the table, then went in search of candles. After going through the kitchen cabinets and drawers, she ended up at the hutch in the dining room. Inside the mahogany cabinet she discovered beautiful china and crystal goblets. She left them alone, but decided to use some napkins from the drawer.

That was when she found the photo album. Her curiosity made her go through the book. The pictures of a much younger Patrick with freckles and a buzz-cut had her smiling. His sisters were all cute, with different stages of hair length and missing teeth. She turned the page and found a picture of a handsome couple. The man was tall and good-looking, with dark hair and eyes. His tall and muscular build was identical to Patrick's. The beautiful woman beside him was tiny and blond, and Cynthia could see so much of Nora in her. These were obviously Patrick's parents.

Suddenly she realized that she wasn't alone. Cynthia turned and saw Patrick. He didn't seem happy to see her.

"Hi," she said. "I didn't hear you come in."

"I wasn't sure if you'd be back or not, since you didn't say a word to me about leaving."

"Kelly told you I was going to be with her."

He nodded. "She did." He was still frowning.

She could see that hadn't appeased him. "Good. I hope you like Italian because I brought dinner home. I was just looking for some candles." She was embarrassed. "I found these pictures."

He walked across the room and shut the album. "There are candles in the kitchen." He put the book back in the drawer and shut it, clearly indicating that he didn't want her nosing into his business.

"I'm sorry, Patrick, I didn't mean to invade your privacy," she told him. He had every right to his secrets, but it still hurt. "You don't have to worry. I won't do it again."

She started to leave when he reached for her and drew her to him. He stared into her eyes, then cursed before his mouth crushed hers. It was a kiss that started hard and deep and just kept coming, consuming her. When he released her, she swayed and had to grip the back of the chair.

"I take it I'm forgiven for my snooping?"

He smiled, but still looked tense. Then he kissed her again.

"I take it you aren't hungry for food?" she asked.

He just cocked an eyebrow and she suddenly lost her appetite…for Italian.

Much later that night they sat on Patrick's bed, at a makeshift dining area on top of the rumpled sheets, eating reheated lasagna. After he and Cyndi had made love, she'd insisted on serving him dinner. He had to admit he was hungry, but after Cyndi pulled on his shirt, he had trouble keeping his thoughts on food. His imagination was working overtime as he looked at her long, smooth legs, especially when she moved and more skin got exposed.

He was about to swallow but his gaze fastened on the one button between her breasts. Their fullness caused a gap in the material, teasing him, making him ache for her again.

"How's your food?" she asked.

"Huh?" He hated that he couldn't seem to think about anything but her. And now that he'd brought her into his bed, he'd never be able to get her out of his head. The way she felt against him, the way she made soft sounds against his ear that made him crazy.

"I asked, how's your lasagna?" she repeated.

"Good." He couldn't taste a thing. "You said you went to the shelter. Did you see Davy?"

"I did." She smiled. "And he asked about you. He said you two talk about guy stuff. It's so sweet that you've taken time with him."

Patrick shrugged. "It's only a few hours a week." The last thing he wanted her to do was make something big out of this. He sure as hell wasn't sweet. Most of the time he was cranky and hard to live with.

"It's more than that. Davy knows you care about him. You've taken time with him. He needs a good male role model." She set her plate on the tray, then reached across and placed a kiss on Patrick's mouth. "You're that man, Patrick Tanner."

"Believe me, I'm far from it."

"I disagree." She studied him. "What about how you stepped in after your parents died? You raised your sisters and somehow managed to run this ranch."

He shrugged and pushed his plate aside. He'd lost his appetite. "You just do what you have to do."

"Do your other sisters live close by?"

"Janie lives in Bend, Oregon, with her husband, Mike, and their son, Brad. She's an elementary school teacher. Karen is an accountant in Salem and married to a good guy named Tom. No children."

"You put the girls through college?"

He shook his head. "They all got scholarships, school loans and jobs. I helped out as much as possible."

"You could have taken the easy road, Patrick, and let them go into foster care." She took another bite of food.

Patrick stiffened. "No, I'd never have let that happen. I wouldn't give the old man that satisfact—" He stopped abruptly.

Cynthia watched Patrick close up as he got off the bed and went to the closet. He took a shirt off the hanger. "I need to check the horses," he told her as he grabbed his jeans off the floor and pulled them on over his boxers. Zipping them, he looked at her. "I'll be gone awhile. You should probably try to get some sleep tonight." With those final words, he walked out of the room.

Cynthia's heart tightened. Suddenly she felt like an intruder. What had changed in a matter of moments? All she had done was ask about his family. Every time she tried to get to know the man, he'd close up and pull away. He definitely didn't want to share personal information about himself.

Just because she and Patrick had shared a physical relationship didn't mean that he wanted more, she reminded herself. The only time he seemed to express any feelings had been when he'd made love to her. It was too late to heed her own warning for caution; she already cared for the man. And she knew he cared about her, too. But he hadn't been foolish enough to fall in love as she had.

Cynthia got up and cleared the dishes from the bed. She smoothed the sheets, where just a short time ago Patrick had made love to her. She felt the tears gather behind her eyes, but she refused to let them fall. After disposing of the trash, she went back to her own bedroom.

Cynthia knew she had to think ahead to life after Patrick. So she concentrated on her trip back to L.A., and her reading for the female lead in *Cheyenne*. An overnighted copy of the script sat untouched on her bedside table. She hadn't had much of a chance to look at it. She'd been too busy with riding and spending time with Patrick.

Normally she put her career first. But for days she'd ignored the script on her nightstand. Sure looked like she would have plenty of time now.

Still wearing Patrick's chambray shirt, she climbed in bed, leaned back against the headboard and turned to the first page of the script. She had a few days to become the young widow, Ellie Brighten, who survived the death of her husband when Indians burned her home, leaving her alone to run the ranch. Somehow, single-handedly, Ellie survives and raises her son and finds love again with another man, Zachary Payne. Everything taken care of in the end.

Cynthia sighed. Only in the movies.

Well after midnight, unable to sleep, Patrick went to the barn so he wouldn't end up knocking on Cyndi's door. He knew he'd hurt her earlier. But it had been the only way he'd been able to let her know that he could never be the man she needed.

He would never give his heart again, never leave himself open to hurt. And he had to stop Cyndi from making him out to be something he never could be.

A long time ago he'd stopped believing in any fantasies of happily ever after. People only ended up hurting each other. Look at his parents, and Gwen.

As a victim of abuse, there was a good chance he'd repeat the scenario and turn out to be like his father. He thought back to the times when he'd lost his temper and barely managed to control his anger.

He drew a long breath. He'd never forget his mother, the terror in her eyes whenever her husband had come home drunk. All the pleading and begging she'd done as Mick Tanner's fist connected with her face.

Oh, God, he never wanted to see that fear in Cyndi's eyes.

Patrick opened the barn door and went inside. The dim lights lined a pathway down the concrete aisle. He went to each gate, checked the occupants and stroked them as he made his way to the end stall. He heard a familiar voice coming from Daisy's quarters. Cyndi.

What was she doing here?

Patrick stood back, not wanting to disturb her, but he couldn't leave, either. That had been the danger of Cynthia Reynolds. He couldn't seem to stay away from her. She'd drawn him in from the beginning, more than any woman he'd ever known.

Cyndi's soft, throaty voice drew him. To whom was she talking? He stepped closer, but stayed in the shadows.

"You don't understand, Zach," Cyndi spoke, then glanced down at the papers in her hand.

A script?

"I can't do this again," she continued. "I can't

let myself rely on another man. Someone who could make me depend on him. Who could make me weak." She paced, her head down. "I loved my husband, and I was so alone after Jake was killed I didn't want to go on." She raised a small, clenched fist in the air as she continued to read to her audience—Daisy.

"My God! I didn't even care about my child, my home—nothing. The pain consumed me so that I wanted to die." Patrick heard tears in Cyndi's voice. "Please, Zachary, understand if I let myself feel again…I'll lose myself. And I never want to feel that helpless again, no matter how much I love you. So I can't marry you, Zachary Payne. I can't. I just can't."

Damn she had him mesmerized.

There was a long silence, then he heard Cyndi blow out a breath. "How'd I do, Daisy?" Her voice was back to normal.

The mare bobbed her head and whinnied softly.

"Oh, Daisy. This is such a great part. I had no idea. I was so busy learning to ride, I forgot the most important thing. The acting. Thanks for your help. Oh, I'm going to miss you," Cyndi said to the horse. "In a million years I never thought that I'd be able to be this close to a horse. Now I can't imagine not riding every day. I'm going to miss you and this place, its beauty and peacefulness. And of course I'll miss Forest, Kevin and Nora."

Cyndi sniffed and wiped her eyes. "And I need you to do me a favor and look after Davy. That little boy needs someone to care about him. And Patrick, too." She patted the horse. "Of course you love him. Who wouldn't love a stubborn, bullheaded, handsome man who takes care of kids and animals? He works too hard and keeps to himself. That's not good."

Patrick hated that she could see through him so easily. Hell, he liked his life. He didn't need anything more. And even if he did, he couldn't give someone like Cyndi what she needed. She would never be happy here…with him.

Before he could get away, Cyndi stepped out of the stall and saw him. She gasped. "Patrick, what are you doing here?"

He tried to act nonchalant. "It's my barn."

Cynthia hugged herself, realizing all she had on was Patrick's shirt and a pair of sandals. He noticed, too. "I meant, I was just surprised to find anyone here."

"You shouldn't have come out here…alone." He nodded to her attire. "Especially dressed like that."

"I wasn't planning on seeing anyone. Just Daisy."

"I'm not angry." He came closer. "I was... worried."

She didn't want him to be nice. "Don't, I'm fine. I've taken care of myself for a long time." She started to go by him, but he stopped her.

"Cyndi, don't go yet."

"Why? So you can walk away from me instead? Go ahead." She motioned with her hand, holding her script. He didn't move.

"I'm sorry if I hurt you earlier."

She ignored his half-assed apology. "I shouldn't have been surprised. You laid it all out for me from the first day. Our relationship was only business." She started off, but didn't get far.

"But I didn't know how much I was going to come to care about you."

She closed her eyes. He'd finally said the words she'd been longing to hear, but too late. Much too late. "Patrick, don't say anything you don't mean."

"It's true. You're the sexiest woman I've ever met." He raked a hand through his hair. "I'm not good with words. I've enjoyed being with you. You've made me laugh and it's been a long time since I've even thought about it. I care about you. I'm just not good at the commitment thing."

"I didn't ask for one," Cynthia said, though she knew she wanted one. Wasn't that what women in love wanted? More than a few days or weeks with this man? But she doubted a lifetime with Patrick would be enough.

"I know you didn't." He came closer. "Do you think we can go back to before? Even if we're just friends?"

She raised an eyebrow. "You want to be friends?"

"If that's what you want."

God that hurt. How could he turn off so completely? "If you don't want me…"

There was a deep groan as he reached for her and drew her against him. "Dammit, Cyndi. Are you trying to drive me out of my mind? Of course I want you. With my every breath."

"Oh," she managed, right before his mouth silenced her. Things were looking up. His tongue swept inside before she could think. But she didn't want to think, only feel. His hands slid down her sides, inch by inch, molding her to him.

She whimpered when his mouth left hers. His gaze locked with hers, relaying his need. He swung her up into his arms and carried her into the stall where they stored bales of hay. "Ever heard the term *a roll in the hay?*"

"What is this NoWait stuff?" Patrick picked the bottle off her dresser the next morning. He'd begun to read the label when Cyndi snatched it away.

"I can't go giving away all my secrets," she told him. They might be sleeping together these past few days, but she wasn't about to confess all her insecurities. "What's my guarantee that you won't sell the info to the tabloids?"

He quirked an eyebrow. "Like that's going to happen." He leaned against the doorjamb, fresh from the shower, wearing a pair of jeans and nothing else. Every girl's fantasy—a near-naked, sexy man in her bedroom.

He came to her. "You don't need anything to enhance your beauty." Those powerful blue eyes searched her face. "I happen to like the natural look." He nodded to the bottle. "What is it? Some miracle oil to take off ten years?"

She felt helpless not to tell him the truth. "Ten pounds," she finally confessed. "It's to help take off ten pounds. That's what the camera adds to my body."

He frowned, then tossed her a slightly crooked grin. "You've got to be kidding. Your body is perfect." His gaze traveled over her, and his hands cupped her breasts through the T-shirt she'd confiscated from him. "See, they fit perfectly." His eyes darkened as his fingers skimmed downward over her stomach. The sensation caused her to suck in a breath as goose bumps rose on her skin. He didn't stop his torturous journey, continuing over her hips, then he splayed his fingers, digging into her flesh, drawing her against his hard body.

She gasped.

"See? We fit perfectly." His head dipped and feasted on her mouth. By the time he ended the kiss, they were both breathing hard.

"I haven't been using it lately," she confessed.

"Using what?" His mouth caressed hers.

"NoWait." She couldn't believe the things he was doing to her. "I haven't been exercising, either."

"Now, I wouldn't say that. We had a pretty good workout last night." He teased her lower lip with his tongue. "And this morning." He deepened the kiss, causing her desire to heighten. With a groan, he released her. "And if I don't show up this morning, Forest will come after me."

He grabbed his shirt off the dresser and slipped it on. After buttoning it, he tucked it into his jeans.

He walked back to her. "You better never play poker, sweetheart. You're too easy to read. And if I wasn't expecting a mare to arrive in about fifteen minutes, I'd give you just what you're asking for with those incredible brown eyes." His gaze intensified as he hugged her to him. "Damn if I don't want you again."

"Well, we seem to have a lot in common, because I want you, too." She kissed him.

He finally let her go. "Take your time getting ready. I won't be finished for at least an hour. We'll go riding then." He sent her a wink and walked out the door.

Cynthia sank onto the mattress and tried to clear her head. She had come here to learn to ride, and she had, but in less than forty-eight hours she'd be going back to L.A. for the audition.

To read for the movie role of a lifetime.

She glanced at the script on the table beside the bed. It didn't seem as important as it once had, before she'd taken the time to find that life had other things to offer, like a man to love.

Patrick finally got Bert Nichols to go home. It had taken him over an hour to assure the man that his mare would be just fine and well cared for while here. He understood Bert's concern, but Patrick found it difficult to be patient when all he could think about was spending time with Cyndi.

He glanced at the house. Was she going to come down and ride? There was only today and tomorrow left. Then she'd be gone. His chest tightened. He knew it was for the best. Even though their time together had been near-perfect. No, it had been perfect. The days…their nights together. His body stirred, but he quickly shook away the feeling. No, it had to end. It was nearly time to move on.

Cyndi would go on location with her movie. He'd stay here and work the ranch, build his vineyard. That was exactly how he wanted it.

"Hey, Pat."

Patrick turned to see Forest coming out to the corral. "What is it?"

"Are you going to be around today?"

"I'm taking Cyndi riding, but we should be close by. Why?"

The foreman shrugged. "Thought we'd planned to move the herd today. Kevin's available this afternoon. The three of us could get it done in a few hours."

Patrick really didn't want to take the time today. "Wouldn't hurt to put it off a few days. Why don't you just go and check out the situation?"

"I could." Forest smiled. "So you want to spend as much time as possible with Cyndi. Can't say I blame you."

As close as he and Forest were, Patrick thought he'd managed to hide a lot from his friend. He should've known better. "She wants to fine-tune some things."

Forest winked. "So that's what you call it." He raised a hand. "Hey, it's okay. Those Reynolds sisters are special. Sexy, intelligent, sexy and funny and beautiful. Did I mention sexy?"

Patrick laughed. "Yes, you did."

His friend sobered. "Cyndi makes you happy. For that, she's pretty special in my book."

"And in two days, she'll be gone."

"But not forgotten," Forest finished for him.

That was the problem. It would take him a long time to forget Cynthia Reynolds. Maybe he never would.

He was brought back to reality when he heard Cyndi call out his name. She was standing at the edge of the corral, dressed in jeans and a blue blouse with that long red hair glistening in the sunlight.

As he had been able to do so many times, Patrick pushed aside his feelings and went to greet her. No, he wasn't going to brood about something that couldn't be changed.

"Hi," she said. Her hands slipped into the back pockets of her jeans. "You want me to saddle Daisy?"

"No." He couldn't resist any longer. He lifted

her in his arms and kissed her thoroughly. When he set her back down, she looked dazed.

"That was… a nice greeting." She looked over his shoulder at Forest. "Aren't we going to ride today?"

He nodded. "Yes, but I thought we'd try something different." He guided her to the barn and Ace's stall. He got a bridle and slipped it on the horse, then walked him out to the corral.

"You've only ridden Daisy. That might not be a good thing because when you start the movie, you'll have to ride another horse anyway. So I thought we'd try you on Ace, who's a little more spirited."

Cynthia was nervous. Ace was bigger than Daisy and he was a stallion. But she trusted Patrick. The man wouldn't let anything happen to her.

"Do you want me to get his saddle?" She started off toward the barn.

"No. I thought we'd go without."

"Bareback?"

"Yeah, it's fun. You can do it."

She loved his confidence. "Okay, what do I do?"

He gave her the reins and showed her how to grip Ace's mane. "I'll give you a boost up." He bent over and laced his fingers together. She placed her booted foot there and easily was lifted up onto the horse.

When Ace shifted under her, she automatically tugged the reins to bring him back. It was strange to feel the warmth of the animal through her jeans. Then Patrick grabbed a handful of the mane and swung up behind her.

"Just pretend I'm not here," he said as his hard body pushed against hers, sending a warm shiver through her.

She glanced over her shoulder to catch his grin. "Like that's going to happen."

"Are you saying I'm bothering you?" His arms circled her waist and brought her closer to him.

She wasn't able to concentrate on the horse. "You're a little distracting."

"Woman, you've been distracting me since the moment I laid eyes on you."

Cynthia smiled as Patrick called to Forest to open the gate and she directed the horse out to the pasture.

She was enjoying the easy stride, feeling every movement of the horse. "Where are we going to go?"

"That's up to you. Anywhere you want. Ace can handle our weight if we don't run him for long."

"I don't think I'm ready to run him at all." She directed the horse to the trail that led to the line shack. For whatever reason, she liked to think about Patrick being there. It seemed like his haven. Maybe she just wanted to create some more memories for him. Good memories that would take away the sadness from his eyes. The sadness that he'd covered with anger to keep people at a distance.

She would give anything to break through that barrier and let her love him.

Ten

Time was running out for them, but Cynthia refused to think about that right now. Their last few
days together had been too perfect and too fragile
to bring up anything about a future.

Cynthia had to accept the present for what it
was. During their short ride to the cabin, she enjoyed Patrick's playfulness, his touches, caresses
and sexy talk. Neither of them brought up her upcoming departure.

By the time they reached the line shack, Cynthia had no doubt that they'd make love. If she

couldn't share his life, she wanted to leave something of herself in a place that was so special to him. She hoped that whenever Patrick came here, he would think of her.

Within seconds of the door closing, they stripped off their clothes. Then Patrick unrolled the mattress on the bottom bunk, spread a blanket, and before he had her on her back, she was in his arms. A giving lover, he made the outside go away. Nothing else existed but his urgent need. His wild mouth and wicked hands coaxed her to behave like a woman very unlike Cynthia Reynolds, to do things she would never do with anyone but Patrick.

When he pulled her beneath him, she saw the depth of desire in his blue eyes, saw the controlled strain on his face. She met his first thrust, wrapped her legs around him, trying to take him deeper and deeper into her soul. He whispered something about how sweet and sexy she was as he began to build the rhythm, increasing her pleasure. Her breathing grew rapid as she climbed higher, then a cry erupted from her throat as she flew apart. A rough sound exploded from Patrick as he joined her journey. Together they soared.

Afterward, Cynthia lay curled up in Patrick's arms. She couldn't seem to stop the tears. Her emotions were crazy. She knew without a doubt that she'd never loved anyone the way she loved Patrick.

His arms tightened around her. "What's wrong?"

She quickly wiped away the tears. "Nothing."

He raised up and looked at her. "Did I hurt you? Was I too rough?"

She took his hand and brought it to her lips. "No, you were perfect. It's just that sometimes afterwards the emotions…just overflow."

His sapphire gaze searched her face. Then he placed his fingers along her cheek. "I never want to hurt you."

She covered his hand. "I know that, Patrick." But he would, when he let her walk away. She placed a kiss on his lips, wanting to be close to him, to shut out the rest of the world for a little while longer. It would invade soon enough. The kiss deepened and his hands began to stroke her again. Their breathing grew ragged and he trailed kisses down her body. She arched her back, selfishly wanting everything from this man, and it wasn't long before she dissolved in pleasure once again.

"Patrick! I love you," she cried out.

She knew that had been a mistake when Patrick pulled away. For a long time there was only silence. She couldn't stand it. "Patrick?"

He didn't look at her as he stood. "We need to get back." He began to slip on his clothes. After shoving his feet into his boots, he headed toward the door. Without turning around, he spoke. "I'll wait outside."

Patrick's hands were shaking so badly he had to dig them into his pockets as he walked to the creek.

She loved him.

He shut his eyes as his heart thudded in his chest. This wasn't supposed to happen. It was only to be a fling, then she'd go on her way, move on with the rest of her life. And he'd have some memories of their unbelievable time together. There weren't supposed to be any lasting feelings, but even he knew there would be. Cynthia Reynolds would be hard enough to get out of his head…and his heart.

Dammit. Why did she have to go and complicate things? There was no way she could be in love with him. She was a famous Hollywood actress.

Not wanting to delve into his own feelings, he retrieved Ace's reins, grabbed the mane and swung up on the animal's back. He turned the horse toward the cabin as Cynthia walked out the door. Her red hair was wild, her eyes glistened and her mouth was swollen from his kisses.

She looked beautiful.

He guided Ace next to the porch and held out his hand. She didn't question him, just took hold and let him lift her up behind him. He sucked in a groan when she scooted up against him, her legs tucked in close, her arms wrapped around his waist, her breasts pressed into his back. He sucked air into his lungs and quickly urged Ace toward home.

"Hang on," he called to her, then he dug his heels into the horse and they took off. The faster he got away from Cyndi the better.

For both of them.

Cynthia had made a big mistake. She'd broken the rules. She'd gotten emotionally involved with Patrick and ruined everything. She opened her suitcase on the bed and began tossing clothes from the bureau inside. Then she went to the closet and began to pull things from the hangers. There wasn't any reason to wait around until she was asked to leave. Besides, she had some pride. She didn't stay where she wasn't wanted, and Patrick Tanner didn't want her here.

She zipped up the bag and glanced around the room one last time. There was nothing left except the NoWait bottle on the dresser. She threw it into the trash, then grabbed her bags and started downstairs. When she made it to the living room, she ran into Nora. So much for sneaking out the door.

"Cyndi." Nora glanced down at the luggage. "I thought you weren't leaving until Sunday."

She had wanted to avoid this. "My plans have changed."

The young woman looked sad. "I guess if it can't be helped… But that doesn't make it any easier to see you go. Are you sure you have to leave right now?"

"I think it's best I stay in town."

"What about Patrick?"

"I've already talked with your brother." But she just recalled she hadn't given him the money. "That reminds me. I need to pay him." She reached into her purse for her check. "Here's what I owe him for the riding lessons."

Nora backed away. "Why don't you put it in his office? I need to check on something in the kitchen."

Cynthia shrugged. "Whatever is convenient."

She went into Patrick's office. Not surprisingly, the room was neat and orderly. A state-of-the-art computer sat on the large oak desk. She placed the check next to the keyboard, but couldn't leave it without a note. She opened the drawer, found a piece of paper and a pen, then scribbled a thank you to Patrick for all he'd done for her. With her hand shaking, and tears threatening, she managed to keep it light and impersonal. She ended by adding her private number. But something told her he would never use it.

Cynthia placed the note under the check, then turned to leave. She gasped when she saw Patrick at the door.

"I was just leaving." She pointed to the desk. "I left your money."

His expression was cold as stone. "I told you I didn't want it."

"And I told you that I don't go back on my word. It's for your services."

He stiffened at her insinuation. "What was between us wasn't a service." He went to the desk and tore up the check. "I don't want your damn money."

"And you don't want me. What *will* make you happy, Patrick, if not my money and not me? What?"

Patrick fought to keep from reaching for her. When she'd said she loved him, he'd nearly exploded with happiness. He wanted to think it was possible. He wanted her so badly he couldn't breathe, but he wasn't foolish enough to believe in happy endings.

"Nothing. I've got everything I want." He turned his back. He needed her to leave now.

No such luck. She came to him. "Do you, Patrick? Do any of us have what we need? I thought I did. I thought my career was all I wanted. When it started to fade, I panicked because it had been my entire life. Yes, I was desperate to get this part in *Cheyenne,* but only because I'd pushed everything else from my life. Then I came here." Her voice lowered. "I met you."

Patrick didn't want to hear her soft, caressing voice. He didn't need to hear about what he couldn't have. He'd had a taste of Cynthia Reynolds, but she could never be his.

He swung around. "We would never work, Cyn. You and I had a great time, but you couldn't be happy here. And I'm not cut out to do the Hollywood scene. I want a quiet life, to watch my grapes grow. To—" He couldn't tell her the real reason.

"How do you know I wouldn't love that life? I've been thinking about a career change. I don't have to go to this audition."

Her big brown eyes searched his for any encouragement. He couldn't give it to her.

"Just ask me, Patrick. Ask me to stay."

She was killing him. "Cyndi, I'm not the man

you want to invest your hopes and dreams in. It's best if you just forget me."

"Why? Why can't I love you, Patrick? You're a good man."

"I'm not. I'll never be what you want."

"How do you know what I want?"

His hands clenched. "Because, dammit! I'm not what any woman needs."

"If you love someone—"

"Love has nothing to do with it." He wasn't getting through to her so he took her by the hand and pulled her into the dining room. He got the album from the drawer and opened to his parents' picture.

"Because of this man, Mick Tanner," he said. "Because he drank—a lot."

"Your father was an alcoholic?"

He laughed. "That's putting it mildly. He was a mean drunk. And when he turned mean, he liked to swing his fists—at his wife in particular. After he beat her, he came after his kids." He glanced down at the photo. "Good old Mick had convinced everyone that he was the perfect family man, but it was all a lie."

Cynthia didn't know how to respond. She hurt for the family, for the children, for Patrick. "Why didn't your mother get help?"

"Each time, he convinced her that it wouldn't happen again. Then later on, when she stopped believing him, he swore he would kill us kids. There were times he probably would have, but I'd taken the girls and hidden them from him."

"The line shack," she breathed. All she could think about was three little girls huddled together, their big brother trying to protect them.

"He came after us once, but he was too drunk to do anything. When we came back home, our mom sported new bruises, a black eye and a swollen lip.

"When I grew older and bigger, I told him that I would kill him if he ever laid a hand on any of us. A friend in the sheriff's department wanted to help, but couldn't do anything unless our mother testified against her husband. She wouldn't. My threats helped some, but the old man still lived in the house. That meant he was still a danger. I worked the ranch while he drank or slept it off."

Cynthia knew that Patrick couldn't have been much more than a teenager himself. "How did you go to school and do all the work?"

He shrugged. "I managed. Then one day I came home and found my mother had fallen down the basement steps. My old man was talking with the police, crying his eyes out about how he'd come in from the barn and found her there. He and I both knew it was a lie, but I couldn't prove it. Lucky for him, he died a couple of years after."

Cynthia watched the pent-up emotions move across Patrick's face. She reached out to him. "Patrick, I'm so sorry."

He pulled back. "I didn't tell you this for sympathy. I told you so you'd know the truth and give up all hope about us. My father was abusive. I was an abused kid, and there's a good chance I'll turn out just like him."

She was shocked. "There's no way that—"

"There's every way. I have a temper. A quick temper."

"You could never hit me or any woman."

"How can you be so sure? According to my mother, Mick Tanner wasn't always abusive." He shook his head. "No, I can't take that chance. It's best that we end this."

"Patrick, I wish I could make you see yourself as everyone else does. Kind and loving. But obviously I can't. You have to work this out for yourself."

Cynthia went to him, seeing the pain in his eyes. She placed a soft kiss on his lips, knowing it would be their last. She wasn't going to change his mind. And she loved him too much to make their parting any harder for him. Any hope they would have a future together was in Patrick's hands.

"What you told me will never change how I feel about you. You're the kindest man I've ever known. I just wish you'd let me help you with your fear. The way you helped me."

Then she walked out, praying he would call to her. But only silence followed her to her car. She didn't have to look around to see if she'd left something behind. She had.

Her heart.

The next morning Patrick watched Nora slam around the kitchen. She might think she was being subtle about her anger, but she wasn't. She'd thought something had been going on between him and Cyndi, and she was disappointed that nothing had developed.

Patrick closed his eyes. *Disappointed* wasn't the word he would use to describe how he was feeling. *Miserable. Pitiful. Rotten.* Those words were more accurate. As much as he wanted to think that Cyndi was just a fling, he knew better. How could he have let the situation get so out of control?

"How could you do that to Cyndi?" his sister finally asked.

"I didn't do anything to her," he lied.

She glared at him. "I'm not a kid anymore, Pat. I saw the sparks between the two of you. The way she looked when she left here, I doubt she was dumping you."

"It was mutual. And for the best. Come on, Nora. She's a Hollywood actress. I'm a rancher."

"You're a great guy. And look around, you're not raising any more kid sisters. It's time for you."

"And I've raised my family. I don't want another." The lies came so easily. So did the pain. So many times he'd imagined a future with Cyndi, her carrying his child. His heart squeezed in his chest. She would be so beautiful pregnant. He swallowed back the dryness in his throat. God, he had to stop this.

"I think that's exactly what you need. Your own family."

"That's never going to happen. So just forget it."

Nora's face crumpled. She looked like she was going to cry. "Sorry I even brought it up," she said.

Patrick stood up. He couldn't listen anymore. "Have you forgotten we have the kids coming out?" He checked his watch. "I've got work to do before they get here. I'll be in the barn." He walked across the kitchen, grabbed his hat and escaped out the door. He needed a distraction, anything to occupy his mind so he wouldn't think about what he couldn't have.

That afternoon, Patrick had just saddled the horses when the shelter bus pulled up. He usually looked forward to the kids' arrival, but he wasn't in the best mood today.

Cyndi had been gone only a few hours and he couldn't concentrate on anything. Maybe it would help if he was distracted by the kids.

Nora came up beside him as the bus door opened and one of the counselors got off, then helped each child out. Today something was different. Every child had on new jeans along with their Tanner Ranch T-shirts. They had on cowboy boots, too, and hats.

He spotted Davy. The seven-year-old grinned and ran to him. "Patrick! I got to come to ride."

"I can see that." He gave the boy a high-five.

"And look. I got a cowboy hat and boots." He stuck out his leg, displaying a shiny pair of black tooled Tony Lama boots. The hat was straw, but good quality.

"Hey, those are sharp," Patrick said surprised. "Where did you get them?"

"We don't know. Someone came to the shelter this morning with a lot of boxes. We got new jeans and shirts and underwear." The boy's eyes widened. "We got new toys, too, and five new computers that are so cool."

"I guess Santa Claus came early," Patrick said, having a pretty good idea who their secret Santa was. Cynthia Reynolds.

"And that's not all. We got camping stuff, too, sleeping bags and tents. So now you can take us on that campout. I need to keep practicing riding to get really good." He looked around. "I gotta tell Cyndi. Where is she?"

Patrick knew the news would break the boy's heart. "She's not here."

Davy's smile faded. "Why?"

Because he'd been a louse and driven her away. "She went back to California."

The boy frowned. "But why?"

"Because that's where her home is."

"She can't go. She said she loved the ranch. She wants to live here."

Patrick looked at a counselor nearby, Betty Moore, to rescue him.

Betty walked up to them. "Davy, why don't you go with Nora? It's nearly time to ride."

The child ignored the counselor and continued to glare at Patrick. "Were you mean to her? Did you make her go away?"

Patrick reached out to the youngster. "No, Cyndi had to go to work on a movie."

"No! She promised she wouldn't leave yet. It's your fault." He swung his fists at Patrick. Though the blows didn't hurt, seeing the tears in Davy's eyes wounded him.

Finally he got his arms around the child. "Stop it, Davy." He tried to hold the boy, but he continued to fight him. That was when Betty stepped in.

"Davy, stop." She grabbed his hands and managed to pull him away and calm him down. "I know you're disappointed, but you can't hit people. I'm sorry, but you've lost your privileges and can't ride today. Please go back to the bus and stay with Rusty."

The sulking boy took off toward the bus and disappeared inside. Patrick wanted to go after him, but he had the other kids to work with today. He walked to the barn, feeling like the biggest heel in the world. He'd broken Davy's heart.

He went over to where the children were lined up, waiting for their turn to ride. Nora and Forest appeared with the first mounts. Patrick put on a smile, but he wasn't in the mood to do this. Somehow, he had to make this up to Davy.

An hour later they'd just finished up with the last of the kids when Betty came running to him.

"Have you seen Davy?"

"No. Not since you sent him back to the bus. Why?"

"We can't find him. Davy told Rusty he had to go to the bathroom. He never came back. We've searched everywhere, but no one's seen him." Betty looked frantic. "I've got to call the shelter."

Patrick glanced at his sister. "Get Forest and Kevin to search the barn and outbuildings."

Nora ran off and minutes later Kevin appeared. "We've already looked in every corner, even the loft."

"Then we need to look further. I'll saddle Ace."

"I'll go, too," Kevin volunteered.

"So will I," Forest said. "We can use our cell phones to keep each other informed."

"What do you want me to do?" Nora asked.

"Take the other kids for cookies as usual. I'll call you with any info." He took off toward the barn.

Nora ran after him as he hurried off toward the tack room. "This isn't your fault, Pat," she told him, trying to keep up with his fast gait. "Davy has problems."

Then why did Patrick feel responsible? "He wanted Cyndi. He thinks I sent her away. And he's right."

Nora shook her head. "He's a little boy. And his life so far hasn't been much."

They could both relate to Davy, since they'd gone through a lot of the same things. "He hasn't been as lucky as I was," she told Patrick. "Janie, Karen and I had you to protect us, to love us. But now that I think back, who was there for you? There was no one to make you feel safe."

Patrick pushed aside her words. "I was older, already an adult. I had everything I needed. Davy doesn't."

Eleven

"So you're giving up?" Kelly asked.

Cynthia knew coming to her sister's had been a bad idea. Instead she should have gotten on a plane and flown back to L.A. Now she had to give Lawyer Kelly the details of her days with Patrick.

"I have no choice. Patrick doesn't want me around."

"What man knows what he wants? Maybe he needs to be convinced that you're for real."

Hadn't she already blurted out that she loved him? "There's only so much humiliation that I can take," she said, trying to fight the tears. But she'd endure it again if she could make Patrick see what a good man he was. "He thinks that since his father was abusive he will be, too."

Kelly handed her a glass of wine, then sat down across the table from her. "Growing up sometimes scars a person. Take me for example. I used to think that money would make me happy. We were so poor growing up, and Mom had been so dependent on men. I never wanted to feel helpless like her. You and I have done everything to avoid falling into that same trap. We've worked hard to be independent, maybe too much so."

Kelly stared across at Cynthia. "We both had had chances with men. Gorgeous men. Rich men. But we both knew we needed more than just looks and money.

"From the first, you fell hard for Patrick and he fell just as hard for you. But you are intimidating, Cyndi. You're an award-winning Hollywood actress, and wealthy to boot."

Cynthia took a long sip of her wine. She didn't care about any of that now. "I'd give it all up for Patrick. I think—no, I know—I could be happy here in Oregon."

Kelly raised her hand. "Don't be so hasty. Why

should you have to give it all up for him? Shouldn't he give something up for you, too?"

She couldn't ask Patrick to live in L.A. She didn't want to live there. "I've been seriously considering going back to school. After being at the shelter, I've been thinking that I want to work with those kids. Just dropping off some money isn't enough."

Before Kelly could reply, the phone rang and she went to answer it. While her sister was gone, Cynthia realized she truly meant what she said. She wanted more from life. She wanted a family. Not having Patrick didn't mean she should give up on her dream. Maybe she couldn't have her man, but there were kids out there who needed love, and one good parent was better than none.

Kelly returned. "That was Nora. It seems that Davy went out for his riding lesson, but he got angry and ran away. Patrick went looking for him."

"I've got to go out there and help." She stood, grabbed her purse and headed for the door.

"Hey, wait for me," Kelly called. "Davy is one of my kids, too."

Cynthia smiled. "Looks like we've both made commitments."

"Yeah, what can I say? Those kids just grow on you."

* * *

After tying his pack on his saddle, Patrick led Ace out of the barn to meet Kevin and Forest beside the corral. They discussed the different directions Davy could have gone. Since the ground was damp from an overnight rain, they were able to find imprints of the child's boots. The tracks passed the fence and headed toward the foothills.

"What area do you want us to take?" Forest asked.

"Since it's still daylight we'll separate. I'll follow the tracks along the trail to the shack. You two sweep on either side of me and see if I miss something. I have a feeling Davy isn't going to make finding him easy." He mounted Ace and looked up at the sky. "If we're lucky we have about three hours of daylight left. Pray the weather holds."

"He knows where the line shack is," Kevin blurted out. When Patrick glared at him, the teenager said, "We talked one day about where to go riding. I said the best trail is to the line shack."

Forest spoke, "Well, if he's smart he'll head there, because rain is forecast before nightfall."

"Then we'd better find him." Patrick set off on the trail, keeping his eyes on the small tracks. As he'd predicted, Davy wasn't making it simple to find him. The boy had zigzagged across the path as if he had no idea where he was going.

Just as Patrick had no idea where he was going. Since Cyndi had left—since he'd sent her away—he'd been lost, too. Patrick slowed his horse along the trail as he went through the tall pines. He listened quietly for any sounds that weren't natural. Since Patrick had grown up in this area, he knew every inch of this land, every hill and ravine. He also knew the dangers of nature and exposure to the elements. Davy was too young to be out here alone.

He was only about a half mile from the shack when he heard a noise. Patrick paused, listening intently, and his eye caught movement. It wasn't on the ground, but up in a tree. He slowed Ace to a walk and studied the area closely. There were several huge pines, some that stood thirty feet high. He glanced upward and saw Davy perched on a limb just above his head.

Patrick sighed in relief and he continued down the trail. He didn't want to let Davy know that he'd been found. First Patrick took out his cell phone and let Forest know to call off the search. The phone reception was poor, but he managed to get across the message that he'd found Davy. Then he rode back for the boy.

"Davy, you can come down now," Patrick said as he rested his arm across the saddle horn.

No response.

"Come on, Davy. I know you're up there, so you might as well talk to me. You have everyone worried. Come down. We have to get back."

"No, I'm not going to. I'm never going back and you can't make me."

Okay, he had a problem. Patrick took out his cell phone and called Nora at the house. "Tell Betty that Davy is safe, but it's going to take a little while to coax him back."

"That's great," Nora cheered. "But you'd better hurry. There's a storm moving in. Where are you?"

"We're about a half mile from the line shack, but he's climbed up a tree. He's pretty upset. I'm going to try and talk him down. Is Betty there?"

"Yeah, I'll get her."

Betty came on the phone. After Patrick convinced her Davy was okay and explained the situation, she asked, "Should I call the sheriff?"

"I wish you wouldn't. Davy is angry with me. I let him down."

She released a long sigh. "That's not true. You've been there for him, Patrick. But sometimes little boys don't understand everything. I trust you to handle him. Keep us informed." She hung up.

Patrick put his phone away and looked up at

Davy huddled in the tree. "Come on, Davy. Why don't you come down and we'll talk?"

"Go to hell."

Patrick released a deep sigh. It was going to be a long night.

With a long sigh, Patrick climbed off Ace and walked the horse to a cleared area just beyond the tree. Off in the distance he saw dark clouds moving in. "Can't get too comfortable," he said to his horse, "because we might have to make a run for it."

He knew he couldn't play games with Davy for long. But he couldn't force the boy to come down; he might fall. He loosened the straps on the saddlebag.

"What are you doing?" Davy called down.

"Ace and I are just getting comfortable. I'm going to let him graze and I'm going to relax." He unrolled the blanket and placed it on the ground.

Patrick sat down and opened his pack. He took out a bottle, took a long pull on the water and sighed loudly. "That sure hit the spot."

He glanced up to where Davy sat, his legs hanging over the side of a large branch. The kid had to be uncomfortable. "Want some?" Patrick asked.

"I told you I'm not coming down."

Patrick stood. "How about if I get you some water?"

"You're just tryin' to trick me," Davy accused.

"No, I wouldn't do that, Davy. I just thought you might be thirsty. I can send up a bottle."

There was a long silence, then Davy asked, "How can you do that?"

Patrick got his rope from the saddle and tied a couple of knots in one end. "When I toss this up, catch it and pull it over the branch."

It took about three tries, but finally Davy caught the end of the rope. "I did it!" he cheered. "What do I do now?"

"You have to pull the rope over the limb so it comes back to me." When the boy did as he asked, Patrick grabbed the other end of the rope, tied on the bottle and sent it up.

The wind swirled through the trees and Patrick could feel the rain in the air. "You know this isn't going to solve anything, Davy. You're going to have to come down sooner or later. You can't just run off when things don't go the way you want."

"What do you care? Anyway, I'm not going back to the shelter."

"I care a lot, or I wouldn't have ridden out here to find you. You have everyone worried."

"Everybody hates me. I cause trouble and get into fights. I just get so mad…."

Patrick could hear the frustration in the child's voice. It broke his heart to listen to the boy. He knew how he felt.

"You've got to learn to control your anger, use it on something else. Because if you don't, it's going to get you into trouble."

"I'm in trouble all the time." The boy's voice broke. "My mom said I was no good—just like my daddy."

Patrick shut his eyes. How many times had Davy heard these words? It doesn't take much for a child to believe the things a parent says. Patrick pushed aside the bad thoughts. It was time he helped rebuild this child's self-esteem.

"You know, Davy, my old man used to tell me I was no good, too."

"He did?"

Patrick stood. "Yeah. I'm going to tell you something if you promise not to tell anyone."

"I promise."

"My dad used to hit me. I wasn't much older than you."

"Does he still hit you?"

"No. But for a long time, I was afraid that he'd come after me. So I kept running away. But until he died I had to look out for my sisters."

"Did he hit Nora?"

"No, I wouldn't let him. I sent them away to hide so he couldn't find them."

"I wish I had you around."

"I wish you had someone to protect you, too. But maybe I'm not the person you think I am." The confession just poured out of him. "I have another secret. I'm always afraid that I'll be just like my dad. That I'll be mean and go around hitting people." ·

There was a long pause. "Did you ever hit a kid?"

"No." He couldn't imagine ever raising his hand in anger, not to a child, or anyone. But there was that possibility with his family genes. That had been the reason he'd always walked away when angry. "No, I don't want anyone to ever feel as bad as I did. You can ask Nora."

"Nora is cool. She's nice to me. I wish she was my sister." He paused and Patrick heard a sniff. "I don't have anybody. So nobody cares if I run away."

"There are a lot of people who care, Davy," Patrick said. "I care a lot about you. I would miss you if I didn't get to see you. Every week, Nora and I keep watch to see if you get off the bus. We were sorry when you lost your privileges."

"They aren't ever going to let me come back to the ranch now."

That was probably true. "Let's not worry about that now. I think you should come down. It's going to be dark in a little while."

The wind swirled around, and the dark clouds made it seem much later than it was. Suddenly another rider appeared on the trail. Patrick recognized Daisy, but knew the rider wasn't his sister. Then he saw the red hair. Cyndi?

What was she doing here?

"Look, Patrick. It's Cyndi and Daisy."

"I guess it is." He wasn't happy that she'd risked her own safety.

The horse and rider stopped by the tree and looked up. "Hey, Davy. I heard you got lost, so Daisy and I thought we'd help find you."

"Cyndi, I thought you went away."

"Not yet."

Patrick walked up beside the horse. "Who let you come out here?"

Cynthia knew Patrick had every right to be upset, but she wasn't going to let him intimidate her. "I didn't ask. I saddled Daisy on my own. I knew Davy would need me."

"I was handling it."

She glanced up at the boy huddled on the limb. "I can see that." She swung down from the saddle.

"In another ten minutes I would have had him down. He trusts me to help him."

A strong gust of wind blew Cynthia's hair, and some big drops of rain hit the ground. "Damn."

"Patrick," Davy called. "I'm getting wet. I want to get down, but I can't."

Patrick's gaze bored into Cynthia's. "It's okay, son, I'm coming to get you." He went to the tree, grabbed both ends of the rope and used it to shimmy up the trunk. By the time he reached Davy, the rain had become heavy.

"I'm glad you came to find me," Davy declared.

"So am I." Patrick swallowed back the dryness in his throat. "Let's just get you out of the rain."

"Okay."

"Put your arms around my neck and I'll get you down."

The boy did as he was asked, and Patrick managed to lower them both to the ground. He carried Davy over to Ace and set him in the saddle, then draped a blanket around him as Cynthia climbed on Daisy and came up beside them.

"There isn't time to make it back to the ranch," Patrick yelled to her as the rain intensified. "We'll head to the line shack. Stay close," he ordered as he climbed up behind Davy.

Cynthia was soaked, but she didn't much care.

She didn't care that Patrick was angry with her, either. What else was new? All she cared about was Davy.

In minutes they reached the cabin. Patrick climbed down, then set Davy on the covered porch. He ordered her to take the boy inside while he secured the horses. Cyndi quickly dismounted and handed him her reins before ushering the soaked child inside the cabin.

He shivered. "I'm cold, Cyndi."

"I know. I'll get you warm in a little while." She went to the bunk and pulled the blanket off the mattress. Intimate memories of her and Patrick's time here flooded back, but she pushed them away. Now she needed to take care of Davy.

Cynthia wiped the water from his face and hair, then draped the blanket around his small shoulders. After seating him on the chair, she pulled off his boots and continued stripping off his clothes until he was down to his underwear. All the while he fought to keep covered by the blanket.

Just then Patrick burst through the door, a pile of firewood in his arms. He went to the stove and opened it. After preparing the wood, he lit a match and the flame caught hold. "Give it a few minutes, and we'll have some heat."

He tossed his hat on the counter, then turned to Cyndi. "Get those clothes off," he barked at her.

Cynthia suddenly realized she was soaked, too. "And put on what?"

Patrick went to the bunk, reached underneath for a box and took out two more gray wool blankets. "Hurry up before you get sick. The temperature has to have dropped fifteen degrees with this front."

Cynthia could hear the heavy rain beating on the metal roof as she sat on the corner of the bunk and took off her boots. When she looked up, Patrick had already stripped out of his shirt. He didn't have a problem walking around half dressed.

"How long do you think we'll be here?" she asked, careful to stay covered with a blanket as she shimmied out of her jeans.

Patrick watched her action and his gaze darkened. "We're not leaving anytime soon. Probably not until tomorrow."

"Wow, that's cool," Davy said. "It's like we're camping."

Patrick wanted to be angry with Davy, but he was too relieved the boy was safe. "Yeah, cool," he murmured as he pulled out his cell phone. People needed to know they were safe and had made it to shelter. When he ended the call, he walked to the window to check out the terrain, but the visibility was nil.

Nightfall would be closing in on them soon and he was trapped with a woman he wanted more than his next breath—and a little boy who needed a few breaks in life.

Around nine o'clock, Patrick's body was begging for sleep. But with Cyndi so close to him it was impossible. He could smell her, could almost feel her heat.

Earlier, he'd been able to distract himself. He'd busied himself with heating up some canned soup and gathering more firewood. He'd strung their clothes on a line, hoping they'd dry before morning. After pulling the mattresses from the bunks and placing them in front of the fire, he knew it was going to be a long night.

At least he'd given Cyndi his undershirt to sleep in so he didn't have to think about her being naked and so close. He groaned. He wasn't going to survive.

With only Davy tucked in between them, how was he supposed to sleep? Not. And listening to her tossing, he doubted Cyndi was doing much better.

"You know," he said, "if you hadn't gone crazy and ridden out here, you wouldn't be sleeping on the floor in a musty cabin."

She rolled on her side and propped her head on her hand, allowing her red mane to fall against her shoulder. "As if I wasn't going to help find Davy," she whispered. "Besides, Nora said he was upset. It was my fault. I know what it's like to have a promise broken."

"It was still foolish," he said, his voice low, not wanting to wake the sleeping child. "You could have been hurt, or fallen off Daisy."

"No one asked you to worry."

Just how was he supposed to stop worrying?

"Besides, I didn't fall off. And we found Davy and he's safe." Cynthia glanced down at the child curled close to her. "We're all safe, Patrick. Tomorrow we'll get back to the ranch and I'll be out of your hair."

"You were never in my hair," he insisted.

Cyndi frowned.

"Okay, maybe at first," he confessed. "It's just that we let things get too personal."

"Kind of like you have with Davy."

She was right. He had let the kid get to him. He'd been thinking about going further and doing something about becoming his foster parent. Yeah, he was going off the deep end, all right.

"I think it's wonderful," she said. "I'm glad someone has gotten to you." She started to turn away, but he reached for her.

God, he hated to see her so hurt. "Cyndi, it's not that I don't care about you… Ah, hell." He placed his hand behind her head and leaned toward her till his mouth met hers. The kiss deepened and raced to the hunger they both felt every time they touched. But Patrick had to be strong, to be the one to let her go. Again.

Cynthia Reynolds was leaving tomorrow. He wasn't going to hold her back, and he wasn't going to make it any harder for either of them.

He heard Davy's voice and released her.

"You're squishing me."

"Sorry," Patrick said. "Didn't mean to wake you."

"That's okay. I wasn't asleep."

There was a long silence, only the crackling of the fire. "Patrick, why did you kiss Cyndi?" the boy asked.

Patrick's gaze shot to the surprised look on Cyndi's face. "I was just saying goodnight."

The rain continued to pound on the roof. "Oh. You like her." Davy giggled. "I like her, too. She's pretty."

Patrick fought a grin, but lost. "Hey, you're too young to notice girls."

Cyndi kissed Davy's cheek. "No, you're never too young for that."

"Now you kiss Patrick," he told Cyndi.

Cyndi looked at Patrick in the dim firelight. "Oh, I think he's had enough kisses."

"No, I could never have enough," he whispered. He leaned over and kissed her softly.

They all settled back against the pillows. It was Davy who spoke. "Cyndi, is it okay to pretend sometimes?"

"Sure," she said.

"Good, because I'm pretending that just for tonight you're my mom and Patrick is my dad."

Patrick's heart tightened. Everything he'd ever wanted was right here. All he had to do was reach out and take it. Instead he turned away before doing something stupid, like blurting out how he truly felt.

Early the next morning all three rode up to the barn as several people rushed to greet them. Kelly was there along with Betty. Davy was fed breakfast while Patrick took the counselor across the room for a discussion.

"I can't thank you enough for finding Davy," she told him. "Of course this means that he'll be losing his riding privileges for quite a while."

"I know that and we'll miss him. Betty, can you tell me, what's Davy's relationship with his mother?"

"There isn't any. She's lost all parental rights."

"His father?"

She shook her head. "He's never been named and no one has come forward. Why the interest?"

Patrick felt his excitement grow. "Just curious." Then he rushed on to ask, "What are the chances of someone like me being a foster parent to the boy?"

Betty looked surprised. "Davy is eligible for foster care, but he's already been sent back twice for being too hard to handle. He seems to test everyone." She smiled. "For some reason, the two of you seem a good match."

Cyndi came into the room wearing fresh clothes that Kelly had brought her. As soon as Davy saw her, he ran into her arms. Every pore in Patrick's body ached as he watched them. She cared about Davy, too.

Patrick turned back to Betty. He knew that he wanted to tell her the truth. "I was abused as a child." He cleared his throat. "Does that still make me a good candidate?"

Betty blinked and for a long time didn't say anything. "Of course. You were a victim, Patrick. I'd say that Davy would be lucky to have you."

Patrick looked at Davy. The kid had somehow gotten under his protective shell. "No, I'd be the lucky one."

Cynthia didn't want to let Davy go. The feeling of him in her arms felt so right, but she had to go. It was clear Patrick didn't want her here. She had to say her goodbyes, then catch her plane for L.A. to meet with the movie director.

With a promise to call Davy and to write, she gave him one last kiss. "You have to promise me you aren't going to run away ever again."

The boy nodded. "I already promised Patrick. He said saying bad words and hitting people isn't good."

At the mention of Patrick's name she looked up and her heart tripped in her chest as she watched him come across the room toward them.

Tears suddenly clouded her eyes. She hugged the boy for the last time. "Bye, Davy. I'll see you again, I promise."

Before Patrick could reach her, she rushed out of the house. She'd thought she could handle it, but she broke down the second she got in the car. Luckily, Kelly was behind the wheel and drove her away. She didn't know if she'd have had the strength to do this alone.

Silently, Kelly reached over and touched her

hand. "Men can be such louses. It's just too damn bad we can't live without them."

Cynthia knew that Patrick was a good man. He just didn't think he could make her happy.

"It's too bad they can live without us."

Twelve

It was bright and sunny the next morning when Patrick walked outside to the porch. He should enjoy it, but after the past days, the peace and quiet he'd loved so much wasn't welcome any longer. All he could think about was watching Cyndi drive away, and the fact that he'd done nothing to stop her.

How could he? She was heading off to another life. Her career.

His chest tightened around his heart. He'd had the chance, but he'd let it all slip through his fingers. Now Cyndi was gone. He'd realized too late that he needed her desperately. Davy needed her, too.

"Staring down that road isn't going to bring her back."

Patrick turned to see Forest. "I know."

"I could tell you you're a fool to let Cyndi go, but I think you already know that."

"She's probably on a plane to L.A. right now."

"You could have asked her to stay."

"What kind of life could I offer her?"

"A life with the man she loves."

Patrick shut his eyes. "It probably wouldn't have worked."

Forest leaned against the porch railing. "You're probably right. Overnight you would have turned into your father and made her life unbearable."

Patrick glared. "What are you talking about?"

Forest's hazel eyes bored into Patrick's. "Well, isn't that what you're afraid of, turning into your old man? It doesn't matter that you're one of the nicest guys I know—you think your personality is going to change.

"Look, Patrick, my old man wasn't a saint, either. He was driven to succeed. That was all that mattered in the Rawlins family. You had to be number one at everything and screw anyone who got in your way. One day I realized I was turning into a person I didn't like. So I walked away." He smiled. "That was eight years ago. It was the best thing I ever did. I'm not my father because I chose a different path, just like you chose to be a good guy and not a bastard like your old man. If you were, do you think I'd be your friend?"

Patrick remained silent. Over the years he'd worked hard to control his anger, vowing he'd never be like his father. Never use his fists. "There were too many times when I wanted to hit something."

"That's the key word, Pat. *Wanted,* not *acted* on those feelings."

"But what if it changes?" he asked. His heart was breaking. "I'd rather die than hurt Cyndi."

"You raised your sisters and you never laid a hand on them. And Nora adores you." Forest smiled. "I'd hate to be the man who falls in love with her. He'll have a lot to live up to. You're her hero."

Hero? "I was pretty strict with the girls."

"And you were patient, loving and there for them. If there were any of Mick Tanner's traits in you they would have showed up by now."

Patrick studied his friend. His words were like a light going on. Forest was right; he'd hated violence, especially against women. He'd worked to protect his loved ones all his life. And he loved Cyndi.

"I talked with Kelly this morning," Forest went on. "Cyndi hasn't left yet. That should tell you something."

That got Patrick's hopes up. "Where is she?"

"I don't know if I should tell you. I promised Kelly."

Patrick knew he didn't deserve another chance. "I love her," he blurted out. "Dammit. You weren't the one I wanted to hear that."

Forest grinned. "Welcome to the human race."

He hesitated again. "It still would be foolish to go after her. Cyndi has a chance to land this great movie." Patrick began to pace. "And what can I promise her?"

"Who says she can't do both. Besides, Cyndi can handle the struggle for a while until the Tanner Forest Vineyard matures and our label begins to sell."

Patrick shot his friend a look. "That's a ways off."

Forest nodded. "Our goal is in sight. And I've been talking distribution, local and in California."

Patrick gave him an incredulous look.

"If you don't go after what you want, you just might lose out."

Patrick knew his friend wasn't talking about
business. Suddenly dread came over him when he
thought about Cyndi not being in his life. He
wouldn't have much of a life.

"Where is Cyndi?"

"She's going by the shelter to see Davy. Then
she's leaving for the airport from there."

Patrick stopped listening and ran to his truck,
all the time telling himself that everything he ever
wanted was waiting for him at the shelter. Now he
had to keep from blowing it.

Cynthia didn't want to say goodbye to Davy.
He'd had too many people in his life who had left
him already. Somehow she had to convince him
that she was coming back, that she wanted to be a
part of his life. To prove she was serious, she was
going to apply to be Davy's foster parent. But she
already knew that she wanted to adopt him.

It had taken a lot of soul-searching, but she
knew now what was important. A life with Davy.
She wanted a family. A movie career came in a dis-
tant second to the little boy who had stolen her
heart. The only thing she couldn't have to com-
plete that perfect dream was Patrick.

Cynthia walked through the shelter's doors. Another thing she was going to make sure of was that

the other shelter kids didn't go without. She had the money to help them, and soon she would have the time to volunteer her self.

Betty Moore walked out to greet her. "Cyndi, I was surprised to get your call. I thought you'd be on your way to L.A. by now."

"I decided there was something that's more important. I want to talk to you about Davy."

The counselor raised an eyebrow. "Sure. Come into my office." Together they entered the small room. "What about Davy?"

"In a few months, I'll be relocating here to Portland. I want to be close to my sister, and I want to be close to Davy. I would like to apply to be his foster parent." She found her hands shaking. "Kelly said that singles can qualify these days. But in time, if Davy wants me, I want to adopt him."

Betty sat down on the edge of the desk. "Well, this is certainly unexpected."

Seeing the counselor's confusion, Cynthia felt the need to sell herself. "Betty, I want you to know that I'm giving up my acting career. I'll be a stay-at-home mom and will eventually go back to school. Of course, I know Davy will have something to say about this. I mean, maybe he doesn't want me."

"Davy adores you," Betty assured her. "But I have to tell you there is someone else who wants the boy."

Cynthia's heart sank as she forced a smile. "Oh. But that's wonderful for Davy." She could barely get the words past the lump in her throat. "I mean a family... Isn't that what every child wants?"

Just then there was a commotion outside in the hall. "Excuse me." Betty opened the door just as Davy ran by.

"David Cooke, you stop immediately," Betty called to him.

The boy slid to a stop, but defiance showed in his young face. "No! I don't want to stay here anymore."

Cynthia came through the door. "Davy, what's wrong?"

"Cyndi!" The boy threw himself into her open arms. "I thought you went away." Tears pooled in the child's eyes. "I don't want you to leave me. I want to live with you."

Cynthia looked up at Betty. Just then the shelter door opened and Patrick walked in.

"This is getting to be a pretty busy place this morning," Betty murmured.

Cynthia couldn't take her eyes off Patrick. Why did he have to show up? Why now?

He looked at her, but didn't give anything away. He marched to Davy. "What's wrong, son?"

"Everybody hates me because I ran away," the boy told him. "Now *nobody* can go to the ranch and ride this week."

As several other kids and counselors appeared interested in the discussion, Betty had a suggestion for the trio. "Why don't we take this into my office for some privacy?"

Patrick was grateful that he'd found Cyndi, but he wished there was a chance he could talk to her alone. Now, though, they had an upset child on their hands.

This time Cyndi took a seat and cradled Davy next to her in the chair, his head against her chest. Patrick wanted them both so badly, he could barely stand back.

Betty came to Davy. "Davy, would you please go to the play area. I need to talk with Cynthia and Patrick."

Reluctantly the boy got up and walked to the back of the room. He picked up a book and opened it.

Betty sat down on the edge of her desk. "It's so nice to see that you both have taken an interest in Davy." The counselor glanced back at the child. "Especially when he hasn't shown his best side." She turned her attention to Cyndi. "When I told you earlier that someone was interested in Davy, I didn't tell you who it was. It's Patrick."

Patrick watched Cyndi's back stiffen.

"Patrick." Betty smiled at him. "It seems that Cyndi expressed the same interest in Davy."

That got Davy's attention and he came running. "You really want to be my mom?"

Cyndi nodded.

The boy looked at Patrick. "And you want to be my dad?"

Patrick nodded.

"Wow! That's cool!"

Betty reached down and took Davy's hand. "Come on, son, I think the adults need to discuss this. Alone." Reluctantly the boy allowed her to lead him away.

Once they were alone, Patrick decided that he had to say something fast before Cyndi left. "I had no idea that you wanted Davy."

She stood up but wouldn't look at him. "And I thought you were afraid of being like your father."

He wanted to hold her so badly, but fought it. "I was a fool to think that. It took me a while, but I realized I would never hurt a child, or anyone. I was a fool about a lot of things."

She finally raised those brown eyes to his. She looked so beautiful that his chest ached. "What other things?"

He couldn't back down now. Too much depended on him finding the right words. "You. I was wrong about you."

Cyndi clasped her hands together. "What about me?"

"I was afraid of how you made me feel." He released a long breath. "It's been a long time since I let anyone get close. When I did, I ended up getting hurt. It was easier to push you away than to risk that again. But what was worse is that I hurt you."

A tear slipped down her cheek. "I can't make you feel for me what you don't feel. I think Davy will be very happy with you." She started to leave, but he reached out to stop her.

"That's not true, Cyndi. He needs you. We both need you. I never should have let you walk away."

"But you did."

"Because I thought it was best for you."

"I think I can decide what's best for me."

"I know that now." He took another breath. The sound of his pounding heart was all he could hear. "I made a lot of mistakes with us. And I'll probably make a lot more. All I know is that I love you, Cyndi. God, I love you so much I can't think about my life without you."

She blinked in surprise.

"I came here to find you," he continued. "To see if you want to share your life with a rancher and

a seven-year-old boy who need you desperately."
His grip tightened on her arms. "You can still have
your career, but just know there are two guys who
will be waiting for you to come home. Please, I
need to know. Is it too late for us?"

She touched his cheek. "No, it's not too late."

Patrick pulled her into his arms as his mouth
came down on hers. The kiss started out slowly but
picked up momentum. His tenderness was a promise of how much he treasured her, how much he
loved her. More tears filled her eyes.

"Oh, Patrick, I love you so much."

"I was hoping you hadn't changed your mind."
He smiled. "So, will you marry me? Have my
babies?"

She brushed the moisture from her face.
"Babies? You want babies?"

"We don't want Davy to be lonely." He sobered.
"But if you don't want children—"

"Oh, yes, I want your babies. And I'll marry you."
She cupped his face and kissed him again, then
again. They barely heard the door open as Davy returned.

"Hey, are you guys going to get married and be
my mom and dad?"

"That's the plan," Patrick said. "We're just
working out some of the details."

"So, does that mean I get to ride Daisy any time I want?"

"Only if you behave." Patrick tried to look stern. "No more bad words and no more running away."

"Okay, Dad." He glanced at Cyndi. "I'm gonna be the best kid you ever had."

They both knelt down and opened their arms to the child who had shown them how easy it was to give love.

Cynthia had known that first night how to give her man what he needed. Love.

Epilogue

Six days later in Wyoming, Patrick watched Cyndi galloping across the open field, her wild mane flying in the breeze, her hat held in place by a leather chin strap. The beautiful bay mare she rode responded easily to her touch.

She was a natural. He was so proud of his new bride. They'd been married three short days ago in Las Vegas, and he'd insisted they honeymoon in Wyoming so Cyndi could take the second step toward landing her prime movie role. She'd read for the part in L.A. on Monday, and at the director's request had just now shown him her riding skills. Against the Wyoming backdrop which was to be the location of the upcoming shoot, Cyndi had not only ridden well, she looked beautiful. After watching her taking on the character of Ellie Brighten, he had no doubt that she'd get the part in *Cheyenne*.

"Cut," the director yelled. "That was perfect, Cynthia."

Patrick breathed out a sigh. It seemed that as far as the director was concerned, the part was hers. Now it was her choice as to whether she accepted it.

Cyndi climbed down off her horse and gave the reins to the animal trainer, then rushed over to Patrick.

She smiled. "Well, husband, are you ready to start the honeymoon?"

He wrapped his arms around her. "No doubt about it. But when do you start filming?"

"I have time, but I'm not sure that I even want this part. I mean I have a family—"

His finger covered her lips. "Your family wants this for you. We talked about this last night, Cyn. Davy and I can handle this." Even though the boy's adoption was still a ways off, Betty had assured them their chances were good. "The filming is only three to four months, and you'll be coming home on weekends or we'll fly here. Don't make a rash decision because of us. I want you to walk away with no regrets."

She touched his cheek. "Oh, Patrick, I have no regrets."

He swallowed hard. "Oh, lady, you know the right thing to say. But I want you to do this movie. You *are* Ellie Brighten."

"But, I can't ask you—"

He cut her off again. "You didn't ask. I'm your husband and I want to do it for you. If the situation was reversed you would do the same for me. Besides there's all that construction going on at the ranch."

One of the things they had decided on was to use some of Cyndi's money to finance a summer camp for abused kids. There were too many children who didn't have anyone, but at least for two weeks in the summer they would get a lot of attention at the Tanner Summer Camp.

"You'll be back for plenty of time being a full-time wife and mother. I just hope you don't regret giving all this up." He hugged her close. "I mean, you're going to be nominated for an Academy Award for the part of Ellie Brighten."

Cyndi smiled. "Thanks for that vote of confidence, but I'll have no regrets. You and Davy are my family, the most important people in my life. And I'm so eager to get pregnant after this movie is a wrap. So be ready, Mr. Tanner."

He cocked an eyebrow. "I'm willing to do my part to make that happen." He lowered his head and kissed her thoroughly. This woman had saved him. Her love had healed his scars and the pain of his childhood.

"Give me a year," she promised him. "And we'll have a new addition to the Tanner family."

"I love you." His mouth covered hers. Cyndi had given him more than he'd ever dreamed. She'd chased away all the bad memories and they were creating new memories and these were all good ones.

Loving ones.

* * * * *

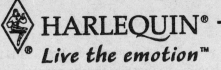